MW01503548

BEFALLEN

The Tragic Hoboken Fires
1973–1982

Dr. Edwin Duroy

Copyright © 2024 Dr. Edwin Duroy
All rights reserved
First Edition

NEWMAN SPRINGS PUBLISHING
320 Broad Street
Red Bank, NJ 07701

First originally published by Newman Springs Publishing 2024

ISBN 979-8-89061-808-5 (Paperback)
ISBN 979-8-89061-809-2 (Digital)

Printed in the United States of America

This book is dedicated to the families who suffered the fires in Hoboken from 1973–1982. Not enough was said or extended to them for their losses during this decade. It behooves us all to remember what happened and look to the future, avoiding tragedies that do not have to exist. The book is also dedicated to the Puerto Rican diaspora, which includes my parents, moving to Hoboken, seeking a better life for their children. Both my father, Paco, a veteran of WWII, and my mother, Manuela, endured challenges in housing and employment but never gave up guiding their five children to receive college degrees.

Finally, I dedicate the book to my wife, Santa, who encouraged me to complete the task of writing the manuscript, submitting it to the publisher, serving as a soundboard during its draft, and keeping me focused with her feedback.

Disclaimer

The interviews presented in the book, although did not directly occur, were based on documented comments, the author's recollection of conversations with the interviewed individuals, and his opinion.

In addition, the Fair Use Act is invoked regarding copyright materials included in the book. The author assumes no responsibility or liability for any errors or omissions in the content of this site, which was prepared in a good faith effort. Further, some names and settings have been changed to respect privacy in this blended genre of non-fiction and fiction novels. In conclusion, Befallen includes graphic photos and the list of actual people lost in the fires as a tribute to their memory.

CONTENTS

Preface..ix

Acknowledgment xiii

Introduction..xvii

Chapter 1   Hoboken 1

Chapter 2   Delia Delgado...5

Chapter 3   The Foodtown Fire 16

Chapter 4   UMASS...21

Chapter 5   The Eleventh Street Fire 28

Chapter 6   *The Boston Globe*.......................................33

Chapter 7   New York City...41

Chapter 8   The 812 Willow Avenue Fire 47

Chapter 9   The *Mirror* 50

Chapter 10   Urban Renewal to Gentrification.............66

Chapter 11   The *Hudson Dispatch* 71

Chapter 12   The Fire of January 29, 1979 77

Chapter 13   Four Fatal Fires 84

Chapter 14   The Markum 93

Chapter 15   Outrage 100

Chapter 16   Vinny 107

Chapter 17   The Proposal 117

Chapter 18   Continuous Conflagration......................125

Chapter 19   The Research 135

Chapter 20   The Interviews................................139

Chapter 21   Lester Beene, Retired FBI Agent.............176

Chapter 22   Jesus Wept 180

Chapter 23   The Homeless Shelter and St.
             Mary's Hospital..............................183

Chapter 24   The Exposé..................................191

Chapter 25   Seeking Justice 206

Epilogue...215

The Befallen...219

References 223

Endorsements..227

PREFACE

Befallen is a creative historic novel comprised of actual events depicting fires in Hoboken, New Jersey, during the late 1970s and early 1980s. The utilization of an eclectic genre allows the reader a more diverse perspective of these real tragedies and creative latitude for the author using a different style of prose. With a young reporter as the protagonist, Delia Delgado, the author captures the tenants' and community's frustrations including feelings of helplessness they experienced of deadly fires in this dramatic retelling saga. Delia describes firsthand the lost lives of neighbors and friends and the destruction of their homes. The fires leave many questions unanswered to this day, evading closure. It chronicles the maturing of a young girl of Puerto Rican background growing up in Hoboken during the 1960s and 70s era of gentrification, and it captures the human side of the consequential events. Delia was considered a "born and raised Hobokenite" attending public schools and the local Catholic church, St. Joseph. After graduating from Hoboken High School, she attended the University of Massachusetts in Boston, studying journalism and media communication, seeking to become an investigative reporter.

At UMASS, she writes for the school newspaper about a major desegregation issue affecting Boston's public schools. As an intern for the *Boston Globe*, she shadows an award-winning reporter, James Walters, who mentors her in writing copy and covering newsworthy stories. She assisted in writing stories about the Watergate saga, the end of the Vietnam War, and the election of a new president, James "Jimmy" Carter. After graduating from UMASS, Delia returns to her hometown in Hoboken, New Jersey, and gets a job in a New York City newspaper company. In the position of junior reporter at Mirror Media Corporation, she participated in the reporting of "Son of Sam" murders in New York City and observed his apprehension. However, faith has its way as she eventually gets a job as a reporter at the *Hudson Dispatch* local daily. This opportunity places her in the middle of a dark time in Hoboken history, the fatal fires of the late 1970s and early 1980s. Covering the deathly fires and the hundreds of smaller fires, she also investigates the cause and effect of gentrification.

The leading causes of house fires in the United States are faulty wiring, cooking accidents, Christmas trees, candles, and space heaters. However, none of these apply to the Hoboken fatal fires. During this short period of time, sixty-seven residents were killed in suspicious fires deemed arson. The National Fire Academy statistics using fire science show that up to 25 percent of all fires in the United States are arson related. What followed the burned tenement fires in Hoboken were sale of properties, renovations, and condo conversions. In an expose, Delia raises poignant questions as to why and who benefited by these tragedies. It takes an intriguing revelation by an insurance investigator who helps Delia and others to confirm that greed and indifference prevail over morality. She leaves us thinking of the unspoken truth of *Befallen*.

A note on the genre: this artistic composition incorporates a diverse range of writing style with the goal of maintaining a focus on the truth. It provides factual, anecdotal, creative, suspective, and firsthand knowledge woven together to arrive at the sad reality of this story.

A Befallen Injustice

The unthinkable act that occurs, violating individuals or group rights, resulting in an inequity.

ACKNOWLEDGMENT

Putting together this saga was possible due to the resources available to the author. The Hoboken Historic Museum brought focus to this issue in several ways. They hosted Dylon Gottlieb, a Princeton University researcher who documented the Hoboken Fires in his paper "Hoboken Is Burning." His public presentation discussing the study at the museum brought the issues the needed stage. The museum also hosted a visual/oral historian Chris Lopez who compiled an art exhibition about the Hoboken fires called, "The Fires: Hoboken 1978–82." These two present-ers were keys to an open conversation about the fires, its impact on the community of Hoboken, and contributed to *Befallen*.

Much of the details about the fatal fires in this book were provided by local media articles from the *Jersey Journal*, *Hudson Dispatch*, *Star-Ledger*, *New York Times*, and the *Hoboken Reporter*. These resources chronicled contem-poraneously the fatal fires as well as the hundreds of fires contributing to thousands of low-income tenants, mainly of Puerto Rican background, to move, or as some stated, escaped the Hoboken fires. The newspapers documented names and addresses of those who died in the fires and thousands affected. Many countless articles provided a sad reality for tenement families living in Hoboken during this period.

Several books were used as references having relevancy to the topic. The book written by Jonathan Mahler, *The Bronx Is Burning*, documented the fires in New York City, which ultimately displaced tens of thousands of families from the Bronx, contributing to the influx of Puerto Rican families to Hoboken. The book *The Power Broker* written by Robert Caro described the governmental authority of planning and the power concept of eminent domain also analogous to Hoboken's renaissance. The book *Yuppies Invade My House at Dinnertime*, edited by Joseph Barry and John Derevlany, offered a window to the controversies and divisions in the community as documented by *The Hoboken Reporter*'s letters to the editor.

In *Befallen*, you will find quotes throughout the book from known authors and others. They include F. Scott Fitzgerald ("Show me a hero..."); Ernest Hemingway ("Courage is grace under pressure"); President Franklin D. Roosevelt ("The Four Freedoms"); Howard Cosell, a sports broadcaster who was quoted during the World Series game as saying, "Ladies and gentlemen, the Bronx is burning"; "Tale of Two Cities" by Charles Dickens; and, finally, Aristotle's quote, "Greed has no boundaries." These quotes contributed to capturing the tragic moments experienced in the Hoboken Fires from 1973–1982.

Additional resources included the Hoboken Fire Department Museum, the documentary film *Delivered Vacant* by Nora Jacobson, Jersey City Public Library, South Amboy Public Library, and the Hoboken Public Library.

The Internet was a valuable resource and facilitated research support for related historic events. Individuals whose conversation, support, and discussions inspired the writing of *Befallen* included my nieces Chantel and Autumn Figueroa and my sisters Edith and Alice Duroy, who faced challenges as Hobokenites of Puerto Rican backgrounds, studied in the public schools, graduated universities, and went on to successful careers. They, like other young women of the 1960s through 1990s, were "Delia Delgado."

Individuals I spoke with in compiling this transcript included Dr. Merry Naddeo, Raymond Perez, Anthony Mestre, Rev. T. Felske, Mario Mercado, Robert Foster, Chris Lopez, Wayne Petretti, Rubin Ramos, Sr., Alice Duroy, Autumn Granage Figueroa, Chantel Figueroa, Blanche Naddeo Fernandez, Santa Duroy, and Donna Rodriquez.

In closing, growing up in Hoboken during this period of time, I was able to witness the tragic fires firsthand. My recollections are reflected in *Befallen* and intended to enjoin in the literature about the Hoboken fires. Finally, the inclusion of definitions and short poems are meant to accent the truth that is *Befallen*.

Fuego!

The fire of tragedy burned the dream in
    my heart
I longed for life's beauty but will never see
Forgotten in time the cries of human cease
Silence comes to those that weep no more
We have died a child's voice
Hope shattered
Smoke filled
The Dream tattered
Who remembers me

INTRODUCTION

Hoboken, 2023

"Maria, let's get a cup of coffee here at Starbucks before we go to the Hoboken Historic Museum up the block."

"Okay, I'm looking forward to seeing the museums' show on the 1978–1982 fires, but I could use a cup of coffee first."

As they entered Starbucks, they were greeted by the barrister who asked, "Can I help you?"

"Yes, I want a grande latte with French vanilla flavor, 2 percent milk, no sugar."

"Is that it?"

"No. What do you want, Maria?"

"I'll have a cappuccino with vanilla flavor, whip cream, and a dash of cinnamon."

"Anything else?"

"No."

"What name?" asked the barrister.

"DD."

"It will be $12.50, DD."

"I'm going to use my Visa card."

"Okay, just tap the card on the machine. Good, it worked. Thank you. You can pick up your order at the adjacent counter. Next!"

"Maria, I never thought that ordering a *café con leche* would be so complicated or for that matter cost as much. The times have really changed since we grew up here."

"Delia, that's an understatement. Did you ever think Hoboken would change as much as it has?"

"No, absolutely not! The city has changed tremendously, especially in housing. I don't want to sound like a senior citizen who only looks back, but I believe to understand the changes you have to regress to an earlier time."

CHAPTER 1

Hoboken

Hoboken is located on the west bank of the Hudson River directly across from New York City. At the turn of the twentieth century, it had become a transportation hub for New Jersey, travel to Europe, and a short subway or ferry ride to New York City. A blue-collar industrial center with many manufacturing companies and corporations, which included Lipton Tea, Standard Brands, Tootsie Roll, Bethlehem Steel, Maxwell House coffee, Wonder Bread, the Holland America cruise lines (travel to Europe), and a vibrant shipping industry. All these industries required skilled and unskilled labor to fill the jobs necessary to deliver the products they produce. The employment demand was filled by European immigrants mainly from Germany, Ireland, and Italy, which comprised the majority of Hoboken residents. However, during WWI, the German population declined.

To many, Hoboken was seen as a rough-and-tumble blue-collar community with a Barbary Coast hosting a concentration of bars on River Street, which serviced sailors, dock workers, and travelers. In 1954, Hoboken was depicted in the movie *On the Waterfront* with Marlon

Brando, an Academy Award picture filmed in Hoboken. It was also known for the hometown of Frank Sinatra, one of the greatest entertainers from the forties until his death in 1998. Sinatra biographers often refer to his early years living in downtown Hoboken section called Little Italy. Last, but not least, Hoboken was known as the birthplace of baseball, where the first organized game was played on Elysian Field, 1846.

During WWI, Hoboken's population grew to over seventy thousand but started to decline after the war. In the 1950s, the population was reduced significantly with the exit of major industries, urban flight to suburbia, and the attractiveness suburban living brought to America. What was left in the city job market was mainly unskilled factory work and a plethora of vacancies in the local tenement buildings in need of repair. The void was quickly filled by the Puerto Rican diaspora. Although being American citizens was an advantaged over previous immigrants, the opportunities in employment and housing were challenging. Conflicts between the Puerto Rican, Irish, and Italian youth was present, perhaps with some similarities to the events in *Westside Story*. The facts were you walked down one block and heard the music of Frankie Valli singing "Sherry Baby" while the next block you heard Willie Colon's trombone in the salsa music playing. Further down the block, sometimes you heard both. Hoboken was truly a conglomeration of neighborhood enclaves that had different cultures living under one roof.

In addition to urban flight, fueling the vacancy rate of tenements buildings was the development of affordable housing by the Federal Housing Authority (The Projects). From 1953 to 1961, they built 840 family units, and another 300 affordable units were built through the Housing Authority called Church Towers. In 1976, the industrial building owned by K & E manufacturing company was renovated into 170 moderate-income apartments. Collectively, the three affordable housing entities built over 1,300 units. Most of the apartments during this period were occupied by residents of Italian and Irish background. On the other hand, the vacant apartments left behind in the neighborhoods were in need of repair but created opportunity for newer residents mainly from Puerto Rican background.

In 1971, the Applied Company, a new development entity, initiated their first project in Hoboken, renovating ninety apartments located three blocks from the Tootsie Roll Company. As such, the block of tenements had been called the Tootsie Roll Flats. Occupied by predominate Puerto Rican families, the vacating of these apartments for renovation initiated the controversy of gentrification. However, the development was part of a federally funded subsidy program resulting in mainly low-income tenants returning to the renovated apartments, an irony contributing to a different perspective toward the company by the community. The company basically adopted the model of acquiring tenement buildings in need of repair, vacating the tenants, renovating, and renting them to low-income families subsidized via federal Section 8 law, a bittersweet paradigm. However, these initiatives played a major role in improving blocks of neighborhoods and also impacted the overall values of Hoboken's real estate. The improvement of neighborhoods enhanced real estate values, and proximity to New York City drew attention with regional media outlets projecting Hoboken as a sleepy alternative to Manhattan without the price. Brownstones, town houses, and rental apartments were available at affordable prices as compared to New York City. It also fueled the beginning of a real estate boom, which turned to gentrification as the catalyst to progress. Hoboken was becoming a bedroom community for middle-class residents, many working in New York City. By contrast, Hoboken also became a nightmare for those residents living in tenement buildings. They feared fires could consume their homes, displace them, and arson would kill them. Hoboken became a city in transition changing from an affordable urban center to a high-end cost of living community. The transition of the 1970s and 1980s made Hoboken a modern-day *A Tale of Two Cities*.

CHAPTER 2

Delia Delgado

Hoboken, a blue-collar community just one square mile, like most inner-city urban communities in the sixties and seventies, was in the midst of urban flight. Once known for its various industries and an import hub with a vibrant commercial shipping center, most followed the move to suburbia and/or other states that offered more accessible locations with lower taxes. What was left behind were minimum-wage jobs in factories seeking unskilled labor, low-income housing in need of repair, and a community poised for change. The local governmental sector was the largest single employer in the city, tied directly to the political machine that doled out the jobs. The city and county government jobs were treated like rewards as part of the political spoils.

The employment opportunities and affordable housing in Hoboken coincided with the migration of Puerto Ricans to New York City from 1950 to 1960. During this period of time, approximately five hundred thousand residents of Puerto Rico moved to New York City seeking a better economic life for their families. Many were veterans from WWII and the Korean War, mainly unskilled but eager to

work, seeking employment. They were able to find manufacturing jobs, become factory workers, and/or worked
in the Manhattan's garment district. Those who did have
trained skills found it difficult to find gainful employment
due to their limited English language and the overt discrimination. Like other ethnic emigrants, they were seeking the
American Dream for their families. However, Puerto Ricans
did have an advantage over the other diasporas since they
were American citizens by birthright as promulgated by the
Jones Act of 1917. Despite the American citizenship, which
granted them the right to vote, discrimination in employment and housing suppressed the community's progress.

In 1955, one young couple from Puerto Rico, like
many others, was seeking to improve their lot in life. Juan
and Elba Rodriquez arrive in New York City's Bronx borough, which housed the largest enclave of Puerto Ricans
in the city, staying at Elba's aunt apartment on the Grand
Concord until they could find employment and housing
of their own. After a week in the Bronx, good fortune did
come to them. They were informed by a neighbor in their
building that a relative, who arrived just three months prior
with the same circumstances, was able to find both housing and jobs in a small New Jersey city called Hoboken.
This was an introduction to what would be a life-changing
move and gave them hope in their outlook.

The following morning Juan inquired from the neighbor as much as he could about Hoboken and how to get
to this oasis. In New York City, the obvious form of transportation was the transit system subways traversing the
entire city and connecting to New Jersey. The A train from

the Bronx would take them to Manhattan's Thirty-Fourth Street, where they would have to transfer to the Hoboken train.

On the following Sunday, ten days from their arrival, they set out to explore the city of Hoboken. Upon arriving in Hoboken, Juan and Elba asked for directions to Garden Street, which was where the Bronx neighbor's nephew lived. They were welcomed into the Gonzalez home by Hector and his wife, Carmen, offering them *café con leche*, a mainstay for a good conversation. The Gonzalez family was living in a one-bedroom apartment and informed that other apartments on Garden Street, not far from where they lived, were available for rent. In addition to the hope for housing, Hector shared that the company he worked for, the Tootsie Roll Corporation, was also hiring. This bright Easter Sunday was truly a blessing.

Juan and Elba set out immediately down Garden Street to find the vacancy signs "Apartment for Rent," an effort that would be repeated by thousands moving to Hoboken. Within two hours of arriving in Hoboken, they had rented a one-bedroom furnished apartment for $75.00 a month. What was left for them to accomplish was jobs for both. They knew they were taking a chance, renting the apartment prior to securing employment, but Juan had sufficient savings of $300.00 from his military severance pay. They returned to the Bronx that evening to gather their belongings for the next day trek back to Hoboken to start their new life.

On Tuesday morning, both Juan and Elba were hired at the Tootsie Roll factory on Fifteenth and Willow Avenue,

Hoboken, for minimum wage of $1.10 an hour. The work week was forty hours, and pay day was every two weeks. Elba would work with other women packing the Tootsie Roll products while Juan was assigned to shipping.

The new Hoboken residents began to settle into the Garden Street apartment and new jobs, walking every morning twelve blocks to the factory, rain or shine. The routine and their ability to save a little something every month coincided with their goal of starting a family. One year from the date Juan and Elba arrived in Hoboken, she was expecting their first child. At six months pregnant, Elba stopped working with Juan's approval. Juan received a raise with a new title, assistant foreman, at $1.25 an hour because he was a veteran and bilingual (English/Spanish). He knew they could survive financially for the short term but needed a larger apartment. On June 15, 1956, Delia Maria Delgado was born at Margaret Hague Hospital in Jersey City.

Four years later, Juan secured a two-bedroom apartment in the housing projects, residing there for ten years. Juan, after losing his job at the Tootsie Roll company when they relocated, was hired by the Applied Company as a maintenance repair worker, which included a new two-bedroom apartment.

By 1970, the overall Hispanic population, mainly Puerto Rican, was as high as 40 percent, occupying tenant apartments throughout the city. During this time period, Tootsie Roll announced their exit from Hoboken followed by Maxwell House Coffee plant and others. The public schools had experienced an increase of students mainly from Puerto Rican background. Delia Marie was one of the new majority. Her parents believed that Delia would have opportunities they did not have growing up, a good education, which would include college. They were both in sync that education would lead Delia to succeed in life.

In elementary school, Delia was a consistent honor student and boosted perfect attendance. This was as a result of her parents' commitment and support. During her years at junior high school, Delia excelled in language arts, becoming one of the best writers in her class and serving as valedictorian of her ninth-grade graduation class. This was the foundation for her success at Hoboken High School as the student editor of its monthly newsletter and her senior yearbook. Her language arts senior teacher, Ms. Martin, recognized her writing and leadership qualities, encouraging her to pursue a career in journalism especially in New York City, the media capital of the United States.

In the spring of 1972, Delia's junior year at Hoboken High School, she wrote about a young investigative reporter who exposed horrendous condition in a mental institution for youth in New York City. The reporter was Geraldo Rivera, a former attorney turned journalist for WABC-TV Channel 7 NYC. On February 2, 1972, WABC-TV aired a documentary produced by Rivera and his camera crew about Willowbrook Hospital in the Staten Island borough of New York City. Delia watched the documentary with her parents and was shocked, like most viewers, to see the conditions the residents of Willowbrook lived under. Willowbrook was a state-operated institution servicing disabled children and young adults whose mental and physical disability needs could not be provided in their homes. Parents, on the most part, gave their disabled children to the state institution for care and safety.

Willowbrook turned out to be the greatest nightmare and injustice faced by the most vulnerable in our society. Rivera brought to light the squalid conditions in the unkempt hospital. The neglected hospital was documented by his tenacity to enter the hospital with his TV crew filming what he had been informed by a former medical staff member. He found children and young adults living in unsanitary conditions replete with filth and misery. Willowbrook was a State institution whose responsibility had overwhelmingly failed the children, families, and society.

Delia was both moved by the documentary and inspired by Rivera's drive to expose a heart-wrenching tragedy. She decided, as a member of the Hoboken High School quarterly newsletter, that she would write an article about Willowbrook and Rivera's commitment to the truth. A week after the program aired, Delia approached the newsletter faculty adviser requesting permission to write the article. She believed the initiative undertaken about Willowbrook was heroic and attributed to a Hispanic role model, Geraldo Rivera. She described how it had an impact on her and how it had inspired her to pursue a career in journalism. Delia's article was well received by both students and faculty.

Delia's senior year at Hoboken High School was the most exciting time as it was a pivotal period in her life including her prom, college selection, and career study.

During the year, she would be part of the school newsletter, senior yearbook staff, and keep a social calendar (a senior passage). Palling around with her best friend, Maria, who she had met in junior high school, they leaned on each other to get through the school year. They both came from Puerto Rican backgrounds, but Delia was Catholic, and Maria was Pentecostal. This distinction was more evident in their social activities outside of school, wherein Maria was not allowed to attend dances or partake in the senior prom.

"Maria, I know you are not attending the senior prom," said Delia. "But can you help me get ready for it?"

As it turned out, the prom was not the most important event in her senior year as perhaps the most important was selecting her college and, of course, getting accepted. Delia had scored 1,030 on her SAT test, with the language arts component being 620. During her senior year, Delia also joined the ASPIRA club, a national nonprofit group that helped high school students, especially of Hispanic background, receive counseling in getting accepted to college. With her ASPIRA counselor, Delia would select the colleges she would apply to based on her career interest.

"What are your career interests?" asked Mr. Colon, her assigned counselor.

"Well, I am interested in a career in journalism, perhaps working in a newspaper, TV, or magazine company. Therefore, I must select a college which has a good program that has ties to media entities."

"You are ahead of the game," said Mr. Colon. "Most students are not as career minded as you. That's good."

Mr. Colon suggested to Delia he would research schools and scholarships to provide her with the appropriate list.

The following week, Mr. Colon provided Delia with three colleges to consider based on her media-career interest including Syracuse University, University of Massachusetts in Boston (UMASS), and Rutgers University in New Jersey. In addition to coinciding with her career ambitions was the fact that they all had financial-aid programs sponsored by the federal government, paying for student tuition and fees. All three institutions had affiliations with media entities; however, UMass had the most attractive package, which included all tuition, board, and fees. They also had an internship program in the junior year at their school of communication affiliated with various media companies located in Boston.

Delia agreed to apply for all three schools, but stated to Mr. Colon, "I will probably accept UMASS if I have the choice because of the internship program at the *Boston Globe* newspaper."

"It's your call, but you need to discuss it with your parents. After all, it means you will be away from home," said Mr. Colon.

"I understand, but it is perhaps what I need to grow. Thanks, Mr. Colon."

By April, her senior year, she had heard from all three colleges notifying her of their acceptance, but she subsequently selected UMASS.

As part of graduation requirement at Hoboken High School, all seniors had to participate in a community-based project. This was an exercise in civics and taught students that they were part of a community and had a responsibility to give back. Some examples of the projects included cleaning a park, tutoring elementary students, and other volunteer projects. Delia was selected to participate in a cleanup project on the Eleventh Street median, which needed cleaning and planting. The site most in need of care was in front of tenement buildings on both sides of Eleventh between Willow and Park avenues. On the fourth Saturday in April, the project was undertaken and completed by the students under the supervision of their teachers; however, little did they know that a tragic event in early fall would change this site forever.

Getting through the college acceptance process, the following month she attended her senior prom with a good friend from her homeroom class, David Hernandez. The prom was all she thought it would be and one of many passages in her life. What was left to the school year was graduation; however, faith and tragedy struck on Memorial Day weekend just four weeks before graduation. A senior classmate of Delia from her homeroom died in a tragic auto accident returning from the Jersey Shore on the Garden State Parkway. Carol D'onofrio, a seventeen-year-old who grew up in Hoboken and, like Delia, was an only child to Joseph and Helen D'onofrio, who were both city employees. It was a very sad day for Hoboken High School and its senior class of 1973.

Delia was very moved by the passing of Carol and decided to organize her homeroom classmates to collect funds for flowers and have them attend the funeral viewing together. At the funeral parlor, the flowers were presented to her parents and the entire class attended. Delia spoke to Carol's parents, saying, "We are all saddened by Carol's passing and wish you and your family to know we will always keep her in our memories."

Mr. and Mrs. D'onofrio were moved by the class attending the funeral and thanked Delia for organizing it. Mr. Charles, the homeroom teacher, praised the entire class the following day and Delia's leadership. Graduation came three weeks after the funeral. Delia as all her senior classmates were excited and anxious to start a major period in their lives. She was soon on her way to Boston while Maria, her best friend, did not pursue college, but rather went directly to the work force. She found employment as a secretary at the local newspaper, the *Hudson Dispatch*, a coincidence not lost to Delia.

Photo Credit: "Miracle Mile Mirror," Tenants
Backyard in Hoboken, New Jersey
1971

CHAPTER 3

The Foodtown Fire

In 1961, a Foodtown market opened its doors on the corner of Third and Jackson Street in Hoboken. It was located directly across the four new Housing Authority buildings called Harrison Gardens. Foodtown had planned their opening with the occupation of the four projects, which housed 188 families adjacent to hundreds of other housing units close by. Foodtown was poised to service these families in the area, most of whom were mainly blue-collar, low-income Italian and Irish backgrounds. Foodtown's origin was a deli market located on First and Park Avenue Hoboken, with products tailored to the Italian community. From this small-size market to a larger one was not a great leap for the Napolitano brothers, but nevertheless a challenge.

Delia's parents, in 1961, moved into the new Harrison Gardens at 310 Jackson Street, directly across from the new Foodtown market. The Delgados were only one of eight Hispanic families living in the four buildings. Delia was six years old when they moved into their new two-bedroom apartment and felt fortunate to be located across from the food market. Delia enjoyed shopping at Foodtown with her parents at least once a week. The other site she loved to go to was the bodega located a block away from their building that carried many Spanish cultural products not present in Foodtown. The bodega sold items such as plantains (*platanos*), dry cod (*bacalao*), rice and beans. It also carried Goya products, a food company mainly serving the Latino community.

In 1966, Foodtown's fifth year, they recognized the neighborhood was changing with an increase of Hispanics in the neighborhood and housing projects. They began to sell products related to the Latino culture and included a section for Goya company products. Basically, the neighborhood ethnic makeup was catered by Foodtown, which became a more eclectic market. Foodtown was a pivotal part of the project area and held the community's support for the first ten years during the 1960s. However, the demographics changed in the neighborhood surrounding Foodtown especially toward the beginning of 1970s when more Latinos and African Americans began to move into the neighborhood. To Delia, Foodtown was an important neighborhood component located in a changing community.

During Delia's junior year in 1972, at Hoboken High School, her father, Juan, had secured a position as a maintenance repairman for the Applied Housing Company. The full-time job included an apartment and the added responsibility to maintain the building hallways clean. The apartment was located at 1207 Williow Avenue, a row of apartment buildings formerly known as the Tootsie Roll flats and the Applied Company's flagship development in Hoboken. However, two weeks prior to moving to their new apartment, Foodtown was destroyed by a fire. Little did Delia know that this fire would have an impact on the community as a whole, ushering the gentrification-by-fire era.

It was a warm evening on Tuesday August 8, 1972, when Foodtown ceased to exist as a community staple and entered the dubious distinction of arson for profit. Once the fire department determined it was arson, it notified the insurance company, which conducted its own evaluation and concurred it was arson. The fire had started around 10:00 p.m. that Sunday night, and although only a few people were out walking around, a young couple, returning from the Pentecostal church evening service, were walking home to their apartment on Third and Jackson Street. They saw a man running from the Foodtown parking area and flames coming out of the building. The couple's attentiveness ultimately contributed to the arrest of an arsonist.

The insurance investigator, Leo Guzman, who was considered an arson and fraud expert, quickly recognized the modus operandi the arsonist used. It comprised of diversion and misdirection by staging a break-in to rob the store's safe using a torch to open it. This ruse suggested the robbery went bad with the torch accidentally lighting paperwork, which was adjacent to the safe, igniting the area and causing the abandonment of the burglary and burning building. However, further investigation of the burned building by the fire department found an accelerant on the other side of the building, suggesting arson. The evidence pointed to insurance fraud; and the method used, along with the description provided by the young couple, led the authorities to a suspect known to the FBI.

The FBI investigation, which had been requested by the insurance company, had identified an arsonist-for-hire from Newark, New Jersey. He was a member of an organized crime family out of Newark that used the same tactic in previous fires, and he met the description provided by the eyewitnesses. Ultimately, he was charged with arson, fraud, and extortion; and the conviction resulted in a six-and-a-half-year sentence, the return of approximately $250,000 insurance money, and a court fine of $3000.00. The owners of Foodtown were responsible for returning the insurance proceeds, although their role in the arson was not established. The conviction represented closure for the insurance company and law enforcement. The FBI was critical in solving the case and subsequently raised questions in the future as to *why* they did not get involved in the fatal fires. The following ten years Hoboken experienced hundreds of arson-suspected fires and the death of sixty-seven residents from 1973 to 1982.

THE STAR-LEDGER, Friday, February 7, 1975

□ 19

CHEWS OUT JUDGE, PROSECUTORS

Arsonist shows court he's hot-tempered

By DONALD WARSHAW
and JOSHUA McMAHON

An underworld "arsonist for hire" exploded with rage in Superior Court yesterday and labeled the judge and prosecutor "a disgrace to the Italians" after being ordered to make restitution of more than $240,000 for a Hoboken supermarket fire.

Frank (the Bear) Basto, 38, of 224 Delavan Ave., Newark, was also ordered by Judge Ralph Fusco to pay $6,000 to a Newark couple who had $6,000 in furs, jewelry and other items stolen from their home.

Basto, a reputed member of the Carlo Gambino crime family, had sat quietly when Judge Fusco handed him a 6½-to seven-year prison sentence for arson in the contract burning of the Foodtown Supermarket at 301 Jackson St., Hoboken, on Aug. 8, 1972.

And Basto remained unmoved when the judge sentenced him to 2½ to three years for conspiracy to commit a breaking and entry at the home of Mr. and Mrs. Robert Ricciardi, 191 Highland Ave., Newark, on Nov. 23, 1972.

* * *

Basto became annoyed, however, when Judge Fusco ordered him to pay a $2,000 fine for the arson plea and a $1,000 fine for the conspiracy to break and enter plea before he could be released from state prison.

And he became enraged when the judge ordered him to make restitution of $241,338 to two insurance companies which had covered the losses in the Hoboken fire and $6,000 to the Ricciardis.

"You, your honor, you're Italian," Basto told Judge Fusco. "The prosecutor is Italian," he said pointing to Assistant Essex County Prosecutor Joseph Falcone.

"You should be ashamed of yourselves. You're a disgrace to the Italians. The Irish are laughing," Basto bellowed.

Later in the day, when Basto was to testify as a defense witness in a stolen coins case in Judge Fusco's courtroom, he refused to sit near Falcone.

"I don't want to sit next to him," Basto said pointing to the prosecutor, while repeatedly shouting a profanity at Falcone and spitting twice in his direction.

And during the trial, Basto shouted profanities at state witnesses, who said they knew him. He said several times, "You never knew me."

* * *

Basto's eruptions caused the judge to revoke his $35,000 bail and send him immediately to the Essex County Jail. Judge Fusco refused to go along with a federal court judge's earlier order that Basto remain free until Feb. 13 to straighten out his affairs.

Basto had pleaded guilty Nov. 27, 1974 to both the arson and conspiracy charges and as a result five other indictments, which included 11 counts of arson and breaking and entering, were dismissed.

Under the agreement, the sentence imposed by Judge Fusco was to run concurrently with a five-year prison term handed down yesterday by U.S. District Court Judge H. Curtis Meanor.

Basto had pleaded guilty last month to the federal charge which accused him and several other men of breaking into the Bamberger's store in Paramus and stealing about $100,000 worth of jewelry.

Basto had allegedly taken the jewelry to Tampa, Fla., and sold it to a local jeweler.

CHAPTER 4

UMASS

On August 15, 1973, at age eighteen, Delia Delgado set out for UMASS Boston campus. She and her parents walked to the PATH train in Hoboken, which would take them to Penn Station in New York City for the train to Boston. This was a momentous occasion in their family's history: the first generation to attend college and Delia's parents' dream for her.

Upon arriving at Penn Station, they went directly to the departing Amtrak assigned track. Tears began to stream from Elba's eyes as it began to sink in—her daughter was leaving them and seeking her lot in life. Juan, on the hand, resisted the emotional moment and was able to give Delia words of advice: "Say no to drugs, don't drink and drive, and remember we love you no matter what." She assured both of them that ASPIRA counselors had trained her and other aspirants the do's and the don'ts. She would also meet up with others from ASPIRA once she arrived at UMASS, which comforted her parents as they said goodbye after hugging her.

Delia's arrival at UMASS was exciting for her knowing that Boston is similar to New York City, and it was a new venture in her life. However, during the early 1970s, Boston public schools were going through desegregation busing crisis, and although it was a concern for Delia and her parents, UMASS assured them that it was not affected by the issue. The university was welcoming to its freshman class during orientation; and she met her roommate for the year, Gloria Lopez, from Pittsburgh, Pennsylvania.

The first month at UMASS was a time to become acclimated to her new surroundings. The freshman year for Delia was a learning experience as she joined the school newsletter staff and was assigned to work at the school library as part of her financial aid package. Her week was full with the sixteen credits she was taking, and what time remained was for study. The adjustment was challenging, but she was up to the task and never thought of letting her parents or herself down.

Boston is a historical center often referred to as the Cradle of Liberty; however, the overriding issue of 1973 was the desegregation crisis. Ordered by the federal and state courts, Boston schools were poised to enter a force busing remedy. It was considered a necessary effort to desegregate the schools an issue generally thought of as a Southern US problem, not the North, although it was a valid issue any part of the country. UMASS hoped to stay above the fray and looked to be supportive in every way they could.

The second item dominating Boston's media was the ongoing Watergate investigation targeting President Nixon's administration. The issue was based on an illegal break-in into the National Democratic Party headquarters in the Watergate office complex, Washington, D. C. From 1972–1973, the nation watched and learned of the presidential abuse of power, ultimately bringing President Nixon to resign in September 1974. Delia, like most Americans, was well versed on the Watergate issue and its implication on the country. The media coverage in print and TV was a plethora of information for the average person in the US society. The *Minuteman*, UMASS monthly paper, editors believed the saturation of information on the topic was plentiful; therefore, they limited its coverage in their periodical.

In the fall of 1973, the UMASS monthly newspaper editorial board chose to feature a series of articles about the Boston schools. Delia, who joined the staff as a student volunteer, was asked by the paper's editor, Jane Thomson, to be part of a committee responsible for writing a comprehensive series covering the issue. She was the only freshman on the committee of four and would prove to be an effective partner. To her, it was very meaningful to participate in the project and a learning opportunity. The committee's charge was limiting the series to no more than three articles, which needed to include interviews of public school students and their families representing both sides of the issue. Writing the legal background on Boston's desegregation issue meant Delia would research available data and articles found readily in the school library where she was working. So between classes, studying, and the library responsibility, she wrote the draft for the committee within a four-week period.

Her second assignment would prove to be more challenging as it required interviewing the African American student selected, James Howard, and his parents. He was the eldest child of four and the only one entering high school. James, who would be an incoming freshman, resided in the Roxbury section of Boston, a predominant Black neighborhood and would be bused to South Boston High School, a predominant White neighborhood. The committee agreed to take no more than three months to complete the articles and begin publishing the series in January. The committee would meet once a week on Saturdays to review the progress of assignments among the four.

The team was charged to document and support articles with factual data and perspectives. Obviously, going home for Thanksgiving and Christmas meant she would be writing the stories while visiting home. Interviewing James Howard and his family was more challenging than the research. Delia and John Riley, the committee leader, were tapped to conduct the interview, visiting them in their home in Roxbury. Delia and Riley needed to initially assure James and his parents that the UMASS newspaper was interested in providing their readers, mainly the college community, with a perspective analysis of students affected by the desegregation issue and pending remedy. James's interview went forward successfully, and his parents were insightful about the issue. What was common in both parents was James's safety despite the overall benefit of busing. Nevertheless, James's parents expressed confidence in the community leaders who had raised the issue of educational inequality and the need to correct it.

As the series draft articles were at the point of completion and reviewed by the committee, it was evident a contrasting view existed among the residents of Boston. The interview of a white student and his family revealed a divide that was festering among Boston families. The busing itself would take place beginning September 1975, but the conflicting views had existed for years. John Brennan and his parents lived in South Boston, a predominantly Irish neighborhood. John was a sophomore at South Boston High School, the elder brother of two elementary school siblings. John, like his parents, expressed concern that all three children would be affected by the desegregation plan, especially if the busing would require the younger siblings being bused, which was not in the present plan. They also raised concerns about safety for John. However, John's parents also recognized the inequality that existed in the Black high school and advocated a remedy along the line of funding but opposed busing.

In January, the UMASS *Minutemen* published the first of three articles on the Boston public school desegregation issue. Delia, as a committee member, had assisted in the final draft written and was flattered to have been part of the series. The articles titled "A Perspective on Desegregation" were well received by the college population at UMASS, who wanted to learn more about the conflict surrounding the community of which they lived. It credited all four participant reporters and received recognition from the college dean, who expressed gratitude for keeping the students and staff informed with three excellently written articles. A letter of kudos received by Delia was framed and forwarded to her parents in Hoboken.

Delia continued to communicate with her parents throughout the year, calling once a week. Her transition from high school to college was indeed challenging, but she was successful in her academic endeavor. By the end of Delia's freshman year, she had completed thirty college credits and partook in writing the desegregation articles on the Boston's public school. She went back home to Hoboken in June for a month hiatus and returned to UMASS for the July-August semester, working at the library.

When Delia returned to UMASS, in the fall of 1974, Watergate was still a major topic. It was an iconic moment in history, crediting two *Washington Post* reporters for bringing down the US president. Robert Woodward and Carl Bernstein, investigative reporters for the *Washington Post*, collected enough evidence to prosecute White House staff and resulted in the president resigning and President Ford pardoning Nixon. Both reporters enjoined in writing a book *All the President's Men*, describing various facets of the case and the use of an informant called Deep Throat.

Early in the semester, Delia wrote an article for the *Minutemen* paper titled "The Effect of Watergate on Our Future." The article emphasized the historic moment UMASS students were living in and the need to learn from this experience. The article received good reviews by the college community as it provided them with a new perspective. *All the President's Men* was on many liberal arts course syllabi reading requirement as it was throughout the country. Delia was inspired by Woodward and Bernstein's heroic courage utilizing their investigative skills. This was more fuel for her to pursue her goal as an investigative reporter.

Delia's sophomore year fall semester included fifteen college credits and work-study assignment at the library again. The desegregation issue was in full gear in Boston, with protesters at public school sites and busing in place. The Watergate saga was winding down with Nixon's resignation and the installing of Gerald Ford as president. However, a new election was underway during the primary season. It represented the second time eighteen-year-olds could vote for president and, for most UMASS students, their very first. The voter registration drive was advocated by the *Minuteman* in every 1974–1975 issue.

The year went fast for Delia, who completed thirty credits and kept her in pace to complete her degree in a four-year period. The summer months were spent on campus, but for June, she returned to Hoboken. Both July and August, she was still working at the library prior to the September *Minuteman* assignment beginning her junior year.

CHAPTER 5

The Eleventh Street Fire

On September 29, 1973, at around 2:00 a.m. in the morning, a fire broke out at 263 Eleventh Street in Hoboken and quickly ignited its adjacent buildings. Four tenements were engulfed in flames and dark smoke, entrapping tenants on the upper floors. The four wood-framed buildings housed some forty families with majority of them being children of Hispanic background. All four tenements suffered irreparable damage gutted by the fire, leaving it fragile and making it difficult for firefighters to bring under control. Residents on the top floors of the five-story walk-up suffered the greatest loss. They were the last to realize the fire, which had burned the lower floors, blocking their exit with flames and smoke. The fire department stated it was arson related, as confirmed by their investigation and identification of an accelerant located on the lower-level stairwell.

In the local paper, *The Jersey Journal*, they described how a father was leading his family toward the back of their burning apartment to utilize the fire escape when he was separated from his wife and children by the billowing smoke. He was overcome by the smoke, losing consciousness on the fire escape and subsequently rescued only to find out his family had perished in the fire. A total of eleven people died early that morning and ten more hospitalized from smoke inhalation. The article ended by describing the sad story of parents trying to save their children and the last moment of life they experienced.

The greatest price of arson is the loss of children, who will never get the opportunity to experience what life has to offer. Of the eleven people who died, six were children, of which five were school age and one age three. They were students at Brandt Junior High and Hoboken High School. They died in the fire along with five adults.

A Puerto Rican community group comprised of activist, bodega owners, and other business leaders convened a meeting with newly elected Mayor Steve Cappiello to discuss the fire. They addressed the city's response time to the fire and how deadly tenement fires of this nature could be prevented in the future. The mayor admitted that the magnitude of the fire was challenging to the fire-department manpower and would study to determine upgrades needed. Secondly, the committee raised the issue of inspections to tenement buildings throughout the city; however, the mayor indicated that the State Division of Housing is the certifying agency requiring inspections only once every five years, an inadequate process. One remedy applicable to fire prevention was the use of smoke detectors; however, only new constructions are required by the state. Finally, the mayor committed to their inspection of tenement buildings with uncorrected violations.

Delia was at UMASS when the fire occurred and heard about it from her mother who said that eleven people were killed. She was familiar with the site, which was in front of the island where she did her senior year community commitment. Eight of the eleven were parishioners of St. Joseph Church, Hoboken, and Father Joseph held a vigil at the site two days after the tragedy. In addition, Father Joseph presided over the funerals of the eight.

The Eleventh Street fire was not the only deadly fire that Delia had experienced living in Hoboken. Six years prior, in 1967, a fire at what was recognized as Frank Sinatra's childhood tenement building on Monroe Street was destroyed, claiming the lives of a grandmother and four of her grandchildren, all of African American background. The Goodwin family lived on the top floor, as did the 1973 victims, in a five-story walk-up wooden frame house. In 1967, Delia was only eleven years old and lived three blocks from the fire; but she remembers the sadness it caused her parents, neighbors, and herself.

The eldest school victim of the Eleventh Street fire was a student at Hoboken High School just two years behind Delia, although she did not know her. Delia's parents, who were active at St. Joseph Church, participated in the community clothing and fundraiser drives to help the displaced families. Additional support was provided by the school counselors for those who were traumatized by the fire and its consequence, an unsung responsible measure.

The Eleventh Street fire, which was clearly identified as arson, never achieved closure although a suspect was identified. By happenstance, a Hoboken police vehicle was passing a block away from the Eleventh Street site when a woman flagged down the detective and informed him that she saw a man carrying what she believed were gas containers into the buildings, giving her the impression he was going to start a fire. As the detective looked up from a block away, he could see flames protruding from the building. He asked the woman to describe the man she saw, and he proceeded to circle the block as he heard the fire trucks approaching the burning building. Within two blocks from the Eleventh Street site, the detective apprehended an individual who met the description given by the witness.

The detective who captured the suspect wrote up the arrest report but was subsequently reassigned before any formal charges were filed. This abrupt assignment change was unexpected and disappointing to the arresting officer. The case was shortly dropped, a mystery to the detective and the beginning of unsolved fire fatality cases.

DR. EDWIN DUROY

10th body sought in fatal Hoboken fire

By JOHN BOGDANSKI

The search continued today in Hoboken for the body of a child believed to be buried in the rubble of an aging five-story tenement at 263 11th St. which erupted in flames early Saturday, killing at least nine persons.

The search units were also seeking evidence of arson. The fire, which quickly spread to three adjoining tenement houses, has been termed "suspicious," but no concrete evidence that it was set had been found at last report.

Six bodies were uncovered by a crane at the site yesterday and three others were found Saturday as state and city police and fire officials combed the debris.

The dead were identified as Carlos Lopez, 32, his wife, Francisca, 55; and three Raquem sisters: Patricia, 19; Jacqueline, 18, and Carola, 16. All were listed as residents of 263 11th St.

The other four bodies recovered were believed to be the wife and children of Dionysio Santos, who is listed in "guarded" condition at St. Mary Hospital, where he is being treated for smoke inhalation and shock.

But police have been unable to obtain positive identifications of the bodies believed to be the Santos family. A police spokesman noted that many of them were charred "beyond any

recognition at all," and one police recovery report said simply: "Unable to tell anything."

Red Cross officials said there might also be another body in the wreckage but that this was "a less than 50 per cent possibility." Because of several parties in progress at the time of the fire, it has been difficult to determine exactly how many persons were in the building, they said.

The interior of the central building in the blaze was so severely damaged by flames, smoke, water and intense heat that fire officials can give only a general picture of where they believe it started.

"It was somewhere in that stairwell," said a fire official as he walked through the fallen debris yesterday. "But what floor it was — the second, the third — you really can't tell. It's such a mess in there."

In addition to Santos, two other residents of the gutted tenement are being detained at St. Mary Hospital. They are Carol Raquem, 17, an Ecuadorian-born student, in "serious" condition, who jumped or fell from a fourth-story window; and Nellie Espesjo, 40, a housewife and mother, who is in "guarded" condition recovering from burns.

Miss Raquem is recovering from second-degree burns. Her

See 10th VICTIM — Page 11

'74 pay bids seen key to county tax

The size of the 1974 Hudson County budget — and the size of...

Hoboken firemen sift through ruins of gutted tenement house at 11th Street and Willow Avenue looking for remains of a child still unaccounted for. At least nine persons lost their lives in the Saturday morning fire, believed to be the worst in the city's history.

Courtesy of the Jersey Journal, Oct. 1, 1973

32

CHAPTER 6

The Boston Globe

The fall of 1975 was Delia's junior year, and she looked forward to an exciting semester as it included the internship with a Boston media company. She was assigned to serve as an intern at *The Boston Globe*, the largest circulating newspaper in New England and over a hundred years in existence publishing a daily periodical. The program would begin in the fall semester with a three-part training component as a full semester of fifteen credits. The first assignment was the finance department, which included budgeting, accounting, advertisement revenue, and payroll. The second part focused on logistics on printing, copy to printing, and distribution logistics. An added element to this component was the technical upgrade, which was in progress via the computerization era. The third and most exciting to Delia was the reporting and editorial division, allowing interns to shadow veteran reporters and observe the editing process. The overall goal of the internship was to introduce and provide the interns with insights of a newspapers' operation from story to print.

Delia began her assignment in the finance division, working closely with the business administrator's office and learning the budgeting process, advertising networking, accountant procedures, and payroll. The component timeline was a total of five weeks in each of the divisions. Initially, she did not understand why it was needed for her to learn the financial component of operating a newspaper since she was interested in reporting, but she came to gain insight as she saw other news companies close due to their economics. The second component was the operation division with printing, distribution, and collection. The art of print layout has been evolving throughout the years from a labor-intensive skilled assignment to a more computerized process. This allowed the editing of print copy by staff to be more efficient and expeditious. Once the print copy was completed and approved, it sequences to distribution. She came away from the operation division with a greater appreciation for the mechanical aspect of the print media.

The third and final internship assignment was working alongside reporters and editors. She was most excited to find herself in this part because it represented her overall goal to become a reporter, especially an investigative reporter. Delia found herself among reporters who just the previous year had won a Pulitzer Prize for covering the Boston public school's desegregation issues. John Mackie led the team that won the award and was also the team-lead reporter working with the interns. By the time she started shadowing the reporter, the main topic at the time was the democratic presidential primaries with the unexpected apparent nominee James "Jimmy" Carter, the former governor of Georgia. His Republican counterpart would be former vice president Gerald Ford, who took over as president after Nixon resigned. Delia wrote about both candidates' working experiences in her articles; however, the greater interest was with Jimmy Carter. For Delia it was yet another learning opportunity at the most exciting time in US history to observe and learn.

During her time at the *Globe*, Delia also came to recognize that sports had a large presence in Boston culture, especially the NBA basketball team the Celtics. In 1973–1974 season, they captured yet another championship, one of twelve in their history, never tiring for their fans. Although the following season was not a championship year, 1975–1976 was poised for another success. The *Globe*, like many large businesses in Boston, were season ticket holders of ten lower-level seats five rows behind courtside, some of the most desired seating in Boston. On October 30, Delia was invited by John Mackie to join them at the Boston Celtic game. It was the first time she attended an NBA game at the famous Boston Garden arena. She experienced a capacity crowd, deafening cheering, and was swept into the euphoria of Celtic victory. As a result of her experience at the game, she penned an article and submitted it to the sports division, describing her presence at the game and becoming the newest Celtic fan for life.

With the junior year coming to a close, Delia prepared to return home to Hoboken and participate in Maria's wedding as a bridesmaid. Maria was getting married in the middle of June to Hector Bonet, a professional electrician who she met at the *Dispatch*. Hector, who grew up a Catholic, convinced Maria and her parents to allow her to be married by the Catholic church since she had grown up in the Pentecostal church. Father Joseph Linski, known as Padre Jose, because he served masses at St. Joseph Church in English and one in Spanish, presided over the wedding. St. Joseph had the largest congregation of Hispanics in the city. Delia, who was a member of the church, had helped to convince Maria to marry at St. Joseph and arranged for them to have their reception at the church hall. It was a great day for the couple and their families and friends.

Remaining consistent as in the other summer months, Delia returned to UMASS for the July/August semester to her work-study assignment at the *Minutemen*. Delia's experience and commitment to the newspaper was rewarded by the editorial staff, who named her assistant editor. Her new assignment gave her the authority to review all articles to be published and edit; however, it was not considered a full-time position as the editor-in-chief, which had a rank of assistant professor and teaching responsibility.

The number one topic during the fall of 1976 was election of president between two candidates, President Ford and former Georgia governor James "Jimmy" Carter. Carter, the Democratic Party nominee, represented himself as the new beginning for the country, moving beyond Watergate. President Ford, who had been appointed vice president by Nixon and replaced him after he resigned, had a greater burden to overcome. Students at UMASS were encouraged to first register to vote and focus on the policy issues that would affect society. The *Minutemen* would publish a pro and con column about the two candidates delineating their positions on issues. Delia oversaw the articles written and approved the copy for print.

The last semester of her senior year meant she would begin seeking employment, "the real world." Fortunately, the University had a placement office that helped its graduates with entry to employment opportunities matching their degree studies. Delia requested information on media companies located in New York City. Employment in New York City was one of her goals and also would be convenient living in Hoboken with her parents. Her parents, Jose and Elba, still lived in the Applied Company two-bedroom unit, where he remained as an employee.

Delia made an appointment for January 15 with the placement officer, Ms. Wellington, and completed an application identifying her career-path goals. Ms. Wellington provided her with a resume packet designed for writing an effective resume along with interview strategies. She also recommended Delia to prepare a portfolio with articles she wrote and/or any recognition she may have received during her years at UMASS. An appointment was scheduled for two weeks to go over the resume and portfolio before any referrals would take place. Ms. Wellington indicated that at that time she would have a list of companies for Delia to consider.

The placement office maintained a network of alumni who worked in various fields and geographic areas throughout the United States supporting their graduating students. For Delia, three media companies located in New York City were selected by Ms. Wellington, which had placed previous UMASS students that met Delia's goal. The three included the *New York Times*, Daily Mirror Media, and the Lester Publishing house. All three entities were located in Manhattan just a fifteen-minute subway ride from Hoboken. The interviews were scheduled for the week of March 10, which coincided with spring break at UMASS.

The first interview was for a position at Lester Media as an assistant book editor requiring reviewing books for publishing consideration. It would also include assisting an editor with their assignments working with new author's book transcripts. The last component and least attractive, Delia would be required to assist in sales of their products including recruitment of new clients. Sales was not a field she was prepared to enter, but since it was her first interview, she did not totally reject the opportunity potential. The interview overall went well with her portfolio presentation and resume. Lester's representative informed Delia that they would make a decision by the following week as they will be interviewing others.

The second interview was scheduled midweek with the *New York Times*, and she recognized it would be the most competitive. The NYT was always looking for new talent; however, they were also known to favor Ivy Leagues applicants especially from Harvard or Yale. Delia presented her portfolio and resume describing her career goal to become an investigative reporter. Perhaps her presentation was an overshot, but Ms. Wellington encouraged her to be candid about goals and demonstrate confidence she would achieve them. She was told by the interviewer that a decision would be made in a week.

The third and final interview would be on Friday with the *Daily Mirror* Media company, which publishes a daily newspaper. They explained to Delia that all new employees would be required to participate in a training program similar to the *Boston Globe*. Employees would be trained in three areas of the paper: the shadowing of reporters, finance review, and operations. Delia presented her portfolio and resume, articulating her goal to become a reporter. Ms. O'Brien, who was the director of personnel at the *Mirror*, was very interested in Delia's presentation and knew she was interviewing at other companies. She informed Delia that they were looking to diversify the employees at the *Mirror* and wanted to expand the papers presence into the Hispanic community in New York City's growing population. "Circulation and revenue," stated Ms. O'Brien, "is important to our existence." In closing, she offered Delia a job at the *Mirror* as a junior reporter, and without hesitation, Delia accepted.

Delia was very happy about getting the job at Mirror Media company and, upon getting home, informed her mother. She also called Ms. Wellington at UMASS that same afternoon to thank her for the referrals and for the inspiration and confidence needed to achieve this key milestone. She subsequently called both Lester Media and the *New York Times* human resource offices to let them know of her decision, withdrawing her application at their companies.

The last two months at UMASS could not go by fast enough for Delia anxiously looking forward to starting her career at the *Mirror* and move back to Hoboken, rekindling with family and friends. Boston was a great experience for Delia, allowing her to grow as a person and preparing her for life. Graduation was May 12, and both her parents would be present for the ceremony. She arranged for them to stay at the downtown Marriott close to the campus. They arrived two days before the graduation in Juan's van so they could help Delia pack her belongings from the dorm. Both Juan and Elba were proud of her accomplishment, receiving her bachelor's degree, a first for their family.

The graduation ceremony brought tears of joy to Delia and her parents who were taking instant photos on the new camera they bought. She was able to see many of her professors and *Minutemen* staff members who attended and thanked them for all their support. Delia took her parents after the ceremony to her favorite restaurant in Boston, the Union Oyster House, for dinner. She had arranged to stay at the Marriott with her parents that night so they could get an early start home, a six-hour drive.

Upon arriving home, she unpacked and called Maria to let her know she would be over tomorrow to see her and her newly born baby girl.

The next two months Delia spent time becoming acclimated again with Hoboken, helping Maria, and preparing for her new job in New York City.

CHAPTER 7

New York City

New York City in the 1970s, like many large urban centers, was in a major decline with crime, with economic downturn ultimately affecting its governance. A subway ride was considered risky, taking in graffiti-filled train compartments. In 1975, financially strapped New York City teetered on the brink of bankruptcy, being unable to meet its fiduciary responsibility. President Ford initially expressed reluctance to help New York City, criticizing its budgetary practice as bloated and was characterized as saying "drop dead NYC." Ultimately, Ford signed a congressional bill to bail out NYC by lending them a $2.3 billion loan for a three-year period.

During this episode in New York's history, close to one million people moved out of the city. Major fires throughout various boroughs, but especially the Bronx, contributed to the exodus. Some nicknames giving to NYC by the media included "fear city," "fire city" and, sarcastically, "fun city." Time Square, considered the center of cultural activities and Broadway plays, was also a gritty crime-ridden area. Yet NYC also served as a center for new music advancements like funk, salsa, hip-hop and disco with its most famous club Studio 54. The disco era also received a major boost as a result of an award-winning movie *Saturday Night Fever*.

In addition to the financial crises, there was a wild-cat strike by the sanitation workers. They walked off their jobs, leaving NYC for two days without garbage collection. "Stink City," yet another negative moniker, was promulgated by the media outlets describing conditions on the streets. Mayor Beame, who served from 1974–1977, faced one crisis after another during his one term. His last year, 1977, would be disappointing, with tenement fires. And on July 13, a two-day blackout of the entire city, caused by lightning strikes to various electrical stations, was dubbed a perfect storm of mayhem. The blackout of NYC brought out the worst looting experience and street fires in its history. Over three hundred stores were looted in the city, with about one-third set afire by vandals. During the two-night blackout, over four thousand looters were arrested, and five hundred police personnel were injured. This melee of events also took place during a murder spree by a serial killer who called himself the Son of Sam. The maladies of the time eventually caused Mayor Beame his job, limiting him to one term.

The blight of the Bronx also drew national attention when President Carter visited the urban center. On October 6, 1977, the president accompanied by city and state officials walked through a Bronx neighborhood along Charlotte Street to experience firsthand the decay. He observed burned-out tenement buildings, empty lots, and squalid conditions that were occupied by Bronx residents. This experience was a sobering one for President Carter, walking through one of the worst dilapidated neighborhoods in America. His visit was described as a welcoming sign of hope for the Bronx in need of much federal support to revitalize the community.

Progress for the Bronx was promised by President Carter, but the reality was, Congress and the bureaucracy operated at their own pace, slow. Subsequently, the laden-filled progress to vitalize the Bronx was used against the president by his opponent in 1980, Ronald Reagan, who criticized the lack of progress. He used a photo taken by him standing in an area similar to where President Carter took his photo on Charlotte Street three years prior. Ronald Reagan's visit to the Bronx was politically motivated and was not repeated during his eight year tenure as president. President Reagan's fiscal conservatism proved less helpful to the Bronx revitalization than Carter's four year.

If New York City had a silver lining, it was Yankee baseball. The stadium was located in the Bronx, and the Yankees were a team whose loyal fans stemmed generations. Expectations for World Series championship fell short in 1976 with their loss to the Cincinnati Reds in four games. The disappointment fit the declining city. However, 1977 would bring the Yankees a second chance at the World Series. Considered by many sports writers as a baseball historic time in NYC, the Series proves to be electric. The dynamic of its new owner, George Steinbrenner; feisty manager, Billy Martin; and the contentious batting star, Reggie Jackson, brought together an energy of success.

An exciting World Series games against the Los Angeles Dodgers was crowned on October 18, 1977, when Reggie Jackson hit three home runs on first pitches and gained the nickname "Mr. October." The Yankees World Series championship euphoria gave NYC a needed boost in the city's aura, making it a pivotal change to an otherwise downtrodden metropolis.

Another notable moment during the second game of the World Series was a comment attributed to the verbose sportscaster Howard Cosell. Cosell, like others, observed and commented that a large fire two blocks from Yankee stadium was burning, making the declaratory statement, "Ladies and gentlemen, the Bronx is burning." This account may have captured the feeling of many New Yorkers who believed major changes to its governance were needed. The Yankees turned the corner to win the series, and New York City followed politically with electing a new mayor, Edward Koch.

The image and reality of the Bronx burning was more evident by the fact that over two hundred thousand residents were displaced by fires, changing demographic tracks in the borough, displacing Puerto Rican families on a disproportional basis. They were families who came here to improve their opportunities and that of their children. Unfortunately, the fires destroyed homes and future aspirations, resulting in thousands of displaced families. The New York City Fire Department and law enforcement authorities suspected arson was the main culprit, resulting in insurance collection by landlords who did not apply the fund to rebuilding. Landlords blamed tenants, although the tenements were not kept up to code and were not held accountable by the city. A community leader was quoted as saying, "Who would want to be part of a diaspora to arrive in the states and burn their own home? No one." This same situation on a smaller scale would repeat itself across the Hudson River in Hoboken, New Jersey.

Fuego! Fire!

During the 1970s and early 1980s, "Fuego, Fire" was the most dreaded words tenants in Hoboken, New Jersey feared the most when they would go to sleep.

CHAPTER 8

The 812 Willow Avenue Fire

On the evening of May 28, 1977, two weeks after Delia had returned to Hoboken and looking forward to start at the *Mirror*, she got a call from Maria that a large fire was raging on Eighth and Willow Avenue, four blocks from her house. Delia decided to see for herself and headed out from her Twelfth Street home, walking down Willow Avenue, toward Eighth Street. Just a block away from her home, she observed the Eleventh Street site where, in 1973, eleven residents were killed in a tenement fire. The buildings no longer existed and were razed by the city because of structural damage and could not be saved for renovation. Instead, what stood in its place was a parking lot operated by the city. Passing by this site toward the fire, she could not help but think whether history would repeat itself for low-income families.

Upon approaching a block away from the burning buildings, Delia saw the firefighters, police, and residents of the area. The community members and neighbors stood staring at homes that were being destroyed, and like them, she felt helpless. Viewing the flames coming out from windows combined with the black smoke contributed to her anxiety. Life for the displaced families were shattered as the place they had called home went up in flames along with their peace of mind, leaving them with an indelible hole in their hearts.

At the fire, Delia spotted John Newton, Maria's boss, standing on the side with his notepad in his hand. She approached him and reintroduced herself.

"Hi, I don't know if you remember me, I'm Delia Delgado, Maria's friend."

"Oh yes, I remember speaking to Maria about you. I understand you are going to work for the *Mirror* in New York City."

"Yes, I guess tonight's fire is probably a sample of what I will be covering for the *Mirror*, but in New York City," said Delia.

"I can tell you it's a noble profession being a reporter with long hours and short pay," responded Newton.

"Sounds great to me," she said.

"You're right. Good luck. I have to get back to my spot watching the fire. Take care."

Returning home after staying at the fire for over an hour, she realized how fortunate it was for her to go home.

The following day she went back to 812 Willow Avenue and saw the extent of the fire, which had spread to the adjacent properties, affecting thirty families, who became homeless overnight. Although eight people were hospitalized, there were no fatalities as compared to the Eleventh Street fire. Newton's article described how residents escaped the burning buildings with some having to jump and others lowering their children from their windows. Fortunately, a firehouse was located around the corner from the fire on Eighth and Clinton Street across from the high school, allowing them to respond quickly, which saved lives.

The following day, Hoboken High School served as a drop-off center for clothes and goods to be distributed to the fire victims along with funds collected by the students.

image via Hoboken Fire Department Memories

Image Courtesy of the Hoboken Fire Museum, 812 Willow Avenue Fire

CHAPTER 9

The Mirror

As Delia became reacclimated with Hoboken life, she began to notice the changes that had taken place in the last four years. One of the most noticeable changes was the housing renovations and construction activities. It was her goal to rent a one-bedroom apartment in the near future after she saved enough money. Related to the goal, she recognized that rental apartments were more competitive and much higher in price since she left for college. In addition, more than before, landlords started to use real estate agents to screen tenants and rent apartments but charged a fee. However, those landlords who rented subsidized apartments did not charge fees but carried long waiting list.

In July 1977, the US economy was experiencing a high inflation rate as well as high interest lending rates, which impacted negatively on the average American business. Nevertheless, these were not the most dominate issue in New York City. It was an obscured set of murders by a killer dubbed as the Son of Sam perpetrating throughout the various boroughs. The killer began his spree in July 1976 using a .44-caliber Magnum gun on seven victims in one year. Panic and urgency prevailed during this period and dominated New York City's print, radio, and TV media daily. It would be a baptism in fire for a new reporter.

Delia started at the *Mirror* on July 11, reporting to the human resources office on the second floor of an eight-story building located on Fourteenth Street. Ms. Helen Sarnoff, the human resource representative, informed her of the assignment as a junior reporter and had her sign a contract with a starting salary of $ 200.00 a week. She was assigned to initially shadow James Landon, a veteran reporter with twenty years under his belt. Landon, a graduate of Boston College, was assigned to cover the murders of Son of Sam, the leading story in New York City. James's daily routine started with checking the board for any information that came from police headquarters on the Son of Sam. He would attend a weekly briefing at One Police Plaza in Manhattan, the headquarters of the New York City Police Department. This was mainly presided by the public information officer for the department and, occasionally, the commissioner especially when a shooting occurred.

Landon briefed Delia on her responsibilities, including attending the weekly briefing with him and follow the reporting by others on the Son of Sam. This monitoring on her part and then reporting to Landon would help him keep up with the latest on the issue. He called it media research. She was to report daily on any new related information in a format designed by Landon outlining TV, radio, and print reporting. He made it clear that the credentials issued to her by the *Mirror* could be used to enter the police briefings and needed to be with her at all times. Finally, she was to be on call 24/7 on the Son of Sam story because it could break at any time, whether the person would be caught or in the event of another shooting.

Delia was excited to be part of an eventful situation covering the Son of Sam murders under the tutelage of Landon. She looked forward to her first briefing at One Police Plaza and experience being part of a larger group of reporters. However, this anticipated event was preempted two days prior by a citywide blackout caused by lightning strikes at three Con Edison sites. The lightning damaged three major stations along the Hudson River north and affected the nuclear power plant Indian Point. The outage lasted for twenty-four hours and brought about major looting of businesses, arson fires, and a state of chaos throughout the city. Over one thousand fires were responded to by New York City Fire Department and contributed to the city's overall malaise.

On Friday, Delia attended her first police briefing meeting Landon outside of the main address to the police headquarters at 8:00 a.m. The briefing was scheduled for nine, but he knew it would be a packed session with not only New York City media, but international press as well. She met Landon at 8:00 a.m. as anticipated and was greeted by him.

"Do you have your credentials?"

"Yes, of course. It was the first thing I did when leaving my house in Hoboken."

"Okay, let's go in," said Landon.

They entered the headquarters and went directly to the press room on the ground level to wait for the press conference to begin. Landon was known by many of the other reporters from print and TV news and was talking to them while Delia waited on the side.

By 9:15 a.m., the press conference began in a room large enough to accommodate approximately one hundred reporters, TV monitors, and technicians. The NYPD press person was to present absent the commissioner, which meant the killings were not resolved or new updates without an arrest. The totals of murders at that point were five with ten wounded by Son of Sam, or his other pseudonym "the .44 Caliber Killer." The NYPD and the mayor were under great pressure to resolve the case and will solve it, exclaimed the press agent. The conference ended with a Q & A lasting twenty-five minutes with reporters shouting questions as the agent exited the room.

Landon and Delia returned to the office writing up the conference details for his copy. Although they both shared their impression of the conference, Landon ultimately wrote the article. She reviewed it, giving him feedback, and also began to understand his writing style. He used the moment to teach her that the articles written need to consider New York City readers' interest and focus. Delia understood this to mean write the article with the main points in the first three sentences with the rest being supportive data. Two articles were written based on the press conference and published on Saturday and Sunday's *Mirror* editions.

The following two Friday's press conferences were basically repeats of the previous one, with no new developments. However, Landon reminded Delia that she needed to remain alert and ready as some ranking police officials he knew let it be known that the department was close to identifying a person of interest. Again, two articles came from each police briefing, and Delia was gaining insight to the development of writing copy. However, little did she know it was the eye before the storm. On Sunday July 31, the Son of Sam struck again, killing one more victim and wounding another. Delia was home when she got a call from Landon, who told her to meet him at One Police Plaza as soon as possible as the police commissioner would be speaking within an hour on the latest shootings.

Delia had her father Juan drive her quickly to the train station where she took the first subway to Lower Manhattan just blocks from Police Plaza. When she arrived at the press conference, it seemed more reporters were present than the last three she attended. The air was thick with anticipation as the commissioner walked in front of the mike.

"Thank you for attending. As many of you already know, there has been another shooting, this time in the borough of Brooklyn, attributed to the Son of Sam. Two young people were ambushed and shot, one fatal and another in critical condition. The details surrounding the shootings have yet to be developed and will follow tomorrow at 10:0 a.m."

There was no Q & A after the commissioner's comments as it ended abruptly, and a somber mood filled the air with his exit.

Delia and Landon returned to the office immediately and wrote the articles, which were credited to Landon. They both agreed to meet the next morning at the police headquarters at 9:00 a.m. for the press conference.

The following day, One Police Plaza conference room had standing room only, with the overflow to the hallway. Commissioner Michael Codd, chief of detectives John Keenan, and the press secretary approached the podium with the press secretary speaking first.

"Good morning. Thank you for being here. This morning both Commissioner Codd and Chief Keenan will be making a statement before Q & A."

First, the commissioner spoke.

"Thank you. Last night, in the borough of Brooklyn, the .44 Caliber Killer murdered one and wounded a second young person. This reprehensible act of cowardice is totally unacceptable to us in the NYPD and the city of New York. Appropriate measures continue to be put in place through-out all boroughs, and we continue to ask the public for your help. As commissioner, I would like to assure all New Yorkers that a maximum number of manpower is working diligently to solve these shootings. Chief Keenan will out-line the effort at this time."

Chief of Detectives Keenan, a seasoned police profes-sional who rose from the ranks, approached the podium to silence from the overflowing crowd wanting to hear every word.

"Thank you. Let me first restate our effort to resolve this case is second to none we ever experienced. A total of 300 police personnel are working on this task, including 75 homicide detectives and 225 police officers. However, the resolution to this case, I believe is with the cooperation of the public, which will help in bringing this nightmare to a close. We are restating the need for the publics' input and reiterate that all leads previously provided were explored and have helped in this process."

At the end of the Q & A, Landon and Delia had the making of three articles of which one would be credited to Delia as the coauthor. The suggestion that input from the public has paid off was accurate, and a person of interest was eminent.

Eight days after the last press conference, Landon received a call from the police press officer indicating that an important announcement was scheduled for the next day, leading him to believe an arrest and perp walk would occur. This meant both Landon and Delia would need to be available from midday on at One Police Plaza, which was expected to be filled with reporters and onlookers.

Delia had never experienced such a tense scene, especially after rumors swirled that an arrest had taken place late morning in Yonkers, New York. The press secretary had scheduled to make a statement at 3:00 p.m. in the crammed conference room that overflowed into the hallway. The conference began on time with Police Commissioner Codd reading a statement.

"Today we are relieved and elated to announce we have arrested a person of interest we believe is the Son of Sam. His name is David Berkowitz, who resides in Yonkers, New York, and works as a postal employee. More details on the arrest will follow at tomorrows' press conference at 9:00 a.m. The investigation and apprehension process needs to be reviewed by the Manhattan prosecutor's office to assure conviction. What can be stated at this time is that the public input played a key role in identifying David Berkowitz.

He has been transported from Yonkers to the Bronx 50th Precinct for questioning and will be transferred and arraigned at 100 Centre Street within the next few hours entering from the South Street garage entrance."

Delia positioned herself to have a clear vision of the garage entrance and assured the *Mirror* photographer had an unobstructed photo opportunity after waiting for four hours. It was 7:00 p.m., and night was setting in. Sirens were heard in the distance. Police had set up barricades leading to the garage driveway as the mass of people awaited with bated breath. Camera lights, flashing light bulbs, and cheers met the police vehicle transporting Berkowitz, who could be seen smiling from the back seat as if he was a rock star arriving at their concert venue. The shooter who had killed six people, wounded eleven others, and terrorized New York City was captured, bringing the nightmare to an end.

Both reporters agreed they had never seen such a scene and knew it could be a once-in-a-lifetime moment in reporting about this event. Landon and Delia wrote four articles together, which appeared in the *Mirror* along with photos of Berkowitz and the Chief Detective Keenan, who had deposed him, recording his confession.

The support provided by Delia was invaluable to Landon's four articles in the *Mirror*, for which he was grateful.

Landon said to Delia, "You have earned your stripes with this experience, and I think you are ready to fly solo as a reporter."

The Mirror had published twelve articles from the point of Berkowitz's arrest to his arraignment. Two weeks after Berkowitz was arrested, the reporting frenzy waned. Delia's shadowing period was ending, and she had to report for the next component of training, a two-week sting on finance and operation. This aspect of her employee preparation would lead to her new assignment as a reporter in a specific division.

After completing her reporter shadowing program, Delia received her new assignment, covering the Bronx borough as her beat. She started with writing about the fires, crime-riddled streets, and displacement of families in her first month as a reporter. The *Mirror* had purposely targeted the Hispanic community and required Delia to write about cultural events affecting the Bronx. This effort was motivated by the need to expand circulation in an underrepresented population. The issue of circulation was important to the *Mirror*'s survival as she learned in her financial training component. The instructor repeated the following to the group several times: "A reporter needs to keep in mind they have responsibility to circulation with their copy." It proved to be pivotal in Delia's future sooner than later.

The *Mirror*, like many newspapers throughout the country, faced financial challenges, although they had done well with the "Son of Sam" and "Yankee" championship coverage. At the end of October, after the Yankee World Series victory, Landon reached out to Delia requesting to meet her after work the following Friday.

He called her to say, "Delia, we need to meet so I can share some important information. Let's meet at McCann's Pub across the street from the *Mirror* on Friday at 5:00 p.m."

"What's up?" she asked.

He simply said, "It's important. I will explain it on Friday. Thanks."

Delia agreed to meet and thanked him for calling.

On Friday after work, she made her way to McCann's Irish Bar and Grill frequented by *Mirror* employees and locals.

"Hey, Landon, how are you doing?" she said after approaching him, giving him a hug and a smile.

"Good, thank you. And you look like a season reporter. I have been following your articles on the Bronx. A tough beat, but I know you can handle it."

"Well, it's definitely challenging but not impossible. Besides you trained me to navigate through tough situations. So what's so important?"

"First, let's order you a drink. I have a beer, and you?"

"I'll have a white wine, thank you."

After exchanging more pleasantry, Landon said, "Delia, I've worked for the *Mirror* twenty years and have seen the success of the newspaper business and its shortcomings. However, I have resigned to take up another job in Burlington, Vermont, where I grew up. The *Burlington Free Press* has offered me to become an editor at the paper."

"Congratulations!" exclaimed Delia. "That's great news. When will you start?"

"In two weeks, but that's not only why I asked you here. It's about the *Mirror*'s future. I have been informed by some friends in finance that layoffs are coming. The *Mirror* is in trouble financially and must let go of people to have a chance of survival. If you are not aware, what usually happens is, last ones in are the first ones out. That would put you on a bad footing."

"I have not been told nor have I heard layoff are coming—well, at least not yet," said Delia.

Landon advised her, "The word is that the *Mirror* will last only six more months even with cutbacks. I just wanted you to have this information so you could prepare for it in advance. You should start putting together your resume and consider applying for a new job in the media industry prior to the layoffs."

"Landon, I don't know what to say, thank you or question you. But I will do both. First, if it's true, I am disappointed that I was not informed about the *Mirror*'s financial problems before being hired. Secondly, I will be going to see Ms. Sarnoff in the human resource office on Monday and ask her about this issue."

"Well, Ms. Sarnoff is not to blame, I am sure she did not know, nor did she see it coming when you were hired. So please don't come down hard on her. Remember she can help with future employment by giving you a good recommendation like I am available to do."

"You're right, I will see her Monday, and if she confirms your information, I will begin sending out my resume shortly thereafter."

"It was wonderful seeing you, Delia. I have to catch a six-thirty train to Vermont with my wife to look for an apartment in Burlington. Take care."

Delia hugged him again, finished drinking her wine, and headed home.

That evening Delia spoke with her mother about the advice given by Landon. Obviously, it was disappointing to Delia, but her mother pointed out she was just getting started in her career, and it is only one of many challenges she would face.

Delia said to her mother, "Ma, it's just I enjoyed working at the *Mirror*."

"I know you do, but as the saying goes, one door closes and another one opens. Don't be totally discouraged, I am sure you will find another job, maybe even better or you could find a rich young man."

"Ma, stop, I told you that's not my priority at this time. I want to achieve success in my career before I get to a relationship. Besides times are different from when you were growing up."

"Esta bien, mija. That's fine, my daughter."

After her conversation with her mother, Delia called Maria for input on the potential layoff. Maria was empathetic and advised her not to make a move until she was sure that layoffs would happen.

"Wait until you go see the human resource person before anything else. You may find out that Landon was wrong."

"I hope you are right, Maria. I like what I'm doing."

Maria encouraged her to keep the faith. "You will be surprised. Pray on it, it works."

First thing Monday morning, Delia called Ms. Sarnoff at human resource requesting a meeting at 3:00 p.m.

Ms. Sarnoff agreed to meet, asking her, "Are you all right?"

"Yes, I will explain when we meet."

The day went by fast, and Delia went to see Ms. Sarnoff, entering her office and greeting her with a smile.

"Thank you for seeing me."

"How can I help you, Delia?" Ms. Sarnoff responded.

"I will get to the point. I spoke to Landon, who told me he was leaving the *Mirror*, but he also told me that the *Mirror* may be considering layoffs because of financial problems. Since I am one of the last ones to be hired, that means I would be one of the first ones to be laid off. Is there any truth to that?"

"Delia, I am not aware that layoffs are pending, and I would be one of the first to be notified as human resource department. But having said that I want to be honest with you, and I know you are aware that a newspaper is a business that relies on revenue to survive. Whether the company is doing fine or not, I am not 100 percent sure. However, regarding the pecking order should layoffs happen, I believe it's a union scenario that seniority does have its priority with exceptions. So what I advise you is that no decision has been made by us at the *Mirror*. I suggest you not make any move to leave as you are a rising star."

The next day, after Delia met with Ms. Sarnoff, she was still not sure what action if any she should take, but nevertheless, she started preparing her resume and as usual she called her friend Maria to talk.

Maria said, "Look, if she told you that layoffs are not pending, I would believe her and would not panic. My thought is to wait and see if anything is pending. At the same time, prepare your resume anyway. Furthermore, I want a copy of your resume so I can hold it should an opportunity present itself here at the *Dispatch*. So drop it off at my house by the end of the week, okay?"

"Yes, okay," said Delia reluctantly.

By week's end, Delia had prepared her resume and aligned it with a portfolio, which included highlights articles and other relevant data in her short but dynamic career at UMASS, the *Globe*, and *Mirror*. She figured to use the portfolio at interviews to enhance her application, but also recognized the resume would only be what gets her the interview.

Returning from work early Friday evening, she stopped at Maria's house to drop off her resume and headed home to her mother's home cooking of *arroz con pollo*.

After dinner, Delia was able to tell her mother about Maria taking the resume to work and presenting it to her boss. Both Elba and Juan were pleased to hear that and suggested it would mean being closer to home and not the problematic Bronx.

"The *Dispatch*," said her father, "could be a good stop and add to your resume for future jobs."

"You're right, Pa. It will probably be a stepping stone, leading me to a more challenging job in the future. *Ojala*, I hope."

Although it appeared to be destiny for Delia to leave the *Mirror*, she took a position of wait and see, continuing to write articles about the Bronx. With the Yankee victory that October, she was asked to write about the prevalent Hispanic neighborhoods that surrounded the stadium. It would include the businesses, its residents, and the fires that surrounded the World Series champions, providing a new perspective on "Tale of Two Cities." Perhaps the largest valued sports club in the world found in the middle of an area known for poverty, unemployment, and tenement fires was a dichotomy of essence. Contributing to this concept of division was the city's celebration of the Yankee victory at Lower Manhattan financial district by holding a ticker-tape parade down the Canyon of Heroes on lower Broadway.

The first week in December, Delia was requested to see Ms. Sarnoff at the human resource office. She had an idea the inevitable had arrived—layoffs. Her anticipation was correct; the *Mirror* was cutting back with layoffs in an effort to survive. Apparently sinking in debt, the *Mirror's* circulation and advertisement revenues had dropped to the lowest level in years. The *Mirror*, like other past newspapers, was on the verge of extinction. Three months into the 1978 year, the *Mirror* ceased to exist, adding to New York City media past history.

Gentrification by Fire

The process of changing the economic composition of a community from a lower to higher income, affecting housing and business settings. The transformation outcome displaces residents of low-income minority groups, seniors, and children on a disproportional basis, with fires as its impetus.

CHAPTER 10

Urban Renewal to Gentrification

To better understand the demographic transformation of Hoboken in the mid 1970s forward, Delia did research on its redevelopment efforts twenty years prior. She found the initial redevelopment was implemented by the urban renewal agency overseen by the Housing Authority. Urban renewal was a federal government strategy designed to convert low-income blighted areas into a more vibrant community but at the expense of removing residents and sometimes businesses in the targeted tracts.

Eminent domain: a legal instrument allowed municipalities, state, and federal governmental authorities to acquire properties identified by professional planners regardless of whether the owners were in accord or not.

The Urban Renewal Agency was utilized in many urban centers throughout the United States including Hoboken.

Hoboken used eminent domain in the late 1940s and early fifties to acquire and assemble land on the western sector for the development of the Federal Housing projects. By the mid 1950s, the Housing Authority built eight hundred units located adjacent to the railroad tracks in a four-square block area. Eminent domain was used again by the Housing Authority when they formally took on the additional role as Urban Renewal Agency, initiating new development including five senior citizen buildings, totaling five hundred additional units.

The Hoboken Urban Renewal agency defined itself by developing affordable low- and moderate-income housing. The moderate-income housing were developed by private for profit and nonprofits entities. Three additional developments processed by the agency were Church Towers (280 units); Marine View Plaza (432 units); and Caparra Homes (40 units), its last development as an agency. The housing development of low-and moderate-income housing was an important strategy to maintain the presence of a diverse community in Hoboken throughout the 1970s to the 1980s.

It became evident to Delia that the Hoboken urban renewal success story was possible because the federal, state, and local governments working collectively to assure affordable housing for its residents. The federal government funded the Housing Authority development for low-income families and its subsidies. In 1969, President Nixon utilized federal tax credits to generate seed money for private developers to construct low- and moderate-income housing, representing a paradigm shift. The federal government would support the development of affordable housing in partnership with the private sector favoring mixed-income projects. The continued effort to construct, renovate, and develop affordable housing extended through the 1970s in Hoboken, in large part by the Applied

Corporation, a privately owned entity. However, with the election of President Reagan in 1980, the federal government strategy changed. It continued to provide support for the existing Housing Authority projects but cut back the Section 8 subsidies for new low-income families and renovated inner-city housing.

The Hispanic community overall indirectly benefited by Hoboken's urban renewal development because it created vacancies in local tenements that had moved into the various new and renovated buildings. The vacancies were filled by families from New York City and directly from Puerto Rico. The federal pivot to private companies developing low- and moderate-income housing also helped these new families, who ultimately occupied approximately 50 percent of the new units developed by the Applied Corporation.

The overall housing improvement effort in Hoboken had a positive impact on the real estate market and housing values, making the development of units more expensive. The national economy was experiencing inflation levels and high interest rates for mortgages needed to purchase homes. The actions of government cutbacks, high inflation, high interest rates, New York crime, and the Hoboken successful redevelopment efforts created a perfect storm for gentrification.

The original concept of federal affordable housing strategy was to provide safe and healthy units for a family generation. This goal was akin to the American dream, providing upward mobility with affordable housing, education opportunity, and the ability of families to succeed in the US society, financially moving out of poverty within one generation. Subsidized housing was not meant to be ad infinitum, and the concept did work for some in the community, but not for all. Because of the inflated housing market and increasing housing prices, most families, including the second generation, were priced out of the market. This left limited choices of either staying in the subsidized units or purchase a home outside of Hoboken that did not have pricing range as high. The financial challenges facing the overall community in Hoboken contributed to the population decline of families, senior citizens, and children. However, nothing accentuated the exodus more than the arson fires of the 1970s.

Delia summarized the gentrification of Hoboken as the removal of low- and moderate-income families. It was direct and indirect efforts motivated by a changing housing market outpricing them. Some viewed the removal of these families as simply collateral damage: they were in the way of progress. She questioned what the price of the Hoboken renaissance was other than gentrification. Turning tragedy to triumph is not a reality. There is no tomorrow for those who perished, but for the survivors, they take with them the love and scars in their hearts. A segment of the Puerto Rican community remains in Hoboken and will always be part of its history.

In her article about gentrification, Delia made an important comparison that runs counter to those who believed fatal fire were directly attributed to low-income minorities or cultural poverty who were prone to fires. She knew that downtown Jersey City was going through gentrification, affecting the residents that happen to be of similar demographic makeup and tenements. Yet the major difference between the two communities was that Hoboken experienced gentrification by fire and Jersey City did not. In her final summary of her article, she stated that both the Housing Authority and the Applied Housing apartments were comprised of low-income families of Hispanic background yet both entities had not suffered any major fires. She attributed this to the buildings' structures, management, and fire-prevention measures.

CHAPTER 11

The Hudson Dispatch

Delia provided Maria with an update copy of her resume and asked her to talk with her boss John Newton. She had hoped the offer made three months ago was still available. Although initially a part-time position, it would allow her to continue serving as a reporter. Opportunities for full-time positions were not good, given the present economy and the fact she only had six months experience. Her last day at the *Mirror* would be December 23, when Maria called to confirm an appointment with Newton at the *Dispatch* for January 3 at 2:00 p.m. to interview for the part-time job. Delia left the *Mirror*, being grateful to have worked there and with a greater appreciation for writing about the Bronx.

On January 3, 1978 Delia met with Newton to discuss her application and brought her portfolio with her, with highlighted articles she wrote going back to *Boston* and the *Mirror*. Newton explained the position available was part-time and paid only $100.00 a week, writing a political column and other ongoing assigned stories. All written stories would need to be approved by his office before being published. In addition, depending upon reporter availability, she could be called on to cover a developing story on weekends if needed. She recognized it was a demotion in her career, but working continuously would help reflect well in her resume. Delia accepted the offer gladly, knowing she would walk to work, not pay for transportation, and be closer to home.

"Yes, I would accept the job. I know it's only part-time, but could it lead to a full-time position?" she asked.

"I cannot guarantee at this time it will. However, the *Dispatch* is looking to expand its circulation among the Hispanic population in Hoboken. I also want to say we at the *Dispatch* would benefit with you joining us based on your education and experience at the *Mirror*."

Delia's starting date was January 15, and she reported first to the human resource office, completing employment papers. She was pleased to accept the position and look forward to starting.

On the first day, she met with Newton to go over her assignment, but Maria first met with her to show her around the office and her desk. Maria walked her into Newton's office and was greeted by him.

"Welcome to the *Dispatch*," he said. "I trust Maria showed you around. I see you have your writing pad, so let's get started. I need you to look up the past two years of political columns on file to get a sense of its tone and scope so you can pick up from where we left off. I have chosen Tuesdays for these columns, because it's our slow day with least circulation. We need to change that, and I think an interesting column on your part will help. How's that for pressure?"

"I'm ready, Mr. Newton."

"Just call me Newton. Everybody else does, okay?"

"What other stories do you want me to cover?" said Delia.

"Before I get to that, I want you to meet Henry Fish. He's the senior reporter and the longest employee at the *Dispatch*, for thirty years. Henry and I have been writing the political column for the past two years and can serve as a good resource should you have any questions."

Henry entered the office and introduced himself, offering to help Delia in any way she needed.

"Thank you, Henry," said Newton as Henry left his office.

Newton also requested that she write some articles about the local Hispanic community, especially Puerto Ricans, which make up the majority. Some of the stories could be about cultural events, issues directly affecting that community, and perhaps about their political role in Hoboken.

The first two days at the *Dispatch*, Delia spent previewing the last two years of the political columns. The year 1977 was a good year for political fodder because it included the election of mayor and council in Hoboken. Apparently, a contentious election took place between Mayor Steve Cappiello and Council Anthony Romano, a former ally to the mayor. Romano, who had run with a Hispanic council candidate on his ticket, fell short to the victorious Cappiello ticket. Cappiello was elected to his second four-year term, advocating for the transformation of the city including the continuation of subsidized housing by the Applied Corporation but also the support of tenement housing conversion into condominiums. His position basically fueled the introduction and expansion of condos in tenement buildings, a concept relatively new to Hoboken but prevalent in New York City.

In her first article, "The Price of Renaissance," Delia talked about the progress made in Hoboken due to the redevelopment efforts. However, it created a negative setting for the low- and moderate-income families who made Hoboken a success story. Hoboken as a community was being touted as a small neighborhood across from Manhattan. Townhouses and brownstones similarly found in New York City were available at a fraction of Manhattan prices. The PATH train to Lower and Mid Manhattan was just one dollar and a fifteen-minute ride. These factors were highlighted in several New York City papers including the Sunday *New York Times*, which carried a large article about the renaissance of Hoboken. This brought visitors from the New York metropolitan area who wanted to see for themselves and found it attractive. She also wrote that real estate brokers and agents began advertising in New York papers such as the *Village Voice* describing Hoboken as an extension of the New York art scene but more affordable. The effort was key to draw newcomers, as they were called in Hoboken.

Beginning in 1978, Hoboken housing stock was considered in play by many real estate agencies. An aggressive effort was underway to get longtime homeowners and tenement building owners to sell their properties. They advanced the idea that vacated buildings would sell for a higher price than occupied ones. Many landlords had seen how the city pressured some tenement owners to sell or face eminent domain. The Applied Corporation was the most to benefit by this action; however, the competitive market made it more expensive to acquire property for affordable units. Again, the pressure was being placed on the landlords to empty their buildings, some believed at all cost.

By the end of 1978, a pattern had emerged for converting tenement buildings into condos. Condo conversion brought in more money for the selling landlords and new developers. The exodus of low-income tenants was most evident in the school district, which had 7,828 students in 1972 and by 1980, the student population was 5,250. Most of the student's population affected by the housing market change was of Hispanic background.

*****

Six months into Delia's tenure at the *Dispatch*, she was hired as a full-time reporter. Henry Fish, the longtime reporter, announced his retirement after thirty-two years of service and, at sixty-two, planned a move to Florida, giving Newton the opportunity to hire her full-time. She welcomed the chance to work as a full-time reporter, allowing her more latitude on her written articles. Her first article was about the demographic shift happening in Hoboken's tenement housing and schools throughout the city affecting their transient rate. One of the more significant population shifts took place in the Housing Authority projects. Once occupied by mainly Italian and Irish background residents, by the end of the 1970s, the majority of tenants were of Hispanic background. The elementary school corresponding to the project area experienced an increase in student population as opposed to the other schools. Connors Elementary school had the largest concentration of minority students in the city at 85 percent. Also contributing to the economic divide, which was growing in Hoboken, the majority of public school students qualified for free meals under the federally funded School Lunch Program. This dichotomy, however, allowed Hoboken to receive additional state aid despite the city's real estate value increasing.

By 1980, Hoboken's opportunity for moderate-income families to purchase a home was slipping away. The acquisition of a home is a mainstay of the American Dream, but it became difficult to obtain a conventional mortgage unless you had a substantial down payment and income. The inflation of home prices coincided with the infusion of newcomers with higher means than many locals. Real estate agencies were setting prices at a higher level simply because it was a sellers' market.

Maria, who worked with Delia at the *Dispatch*, was unable to buy a home in Hoboken because of the pricing and ultimately bought a home in the Jersey City Heights overlooking Hoboken, an example of gentrification.

CHAPTER 12

The Fire of January 29, 1979

The new year in 1979 was a continuation of housing pressure for tenements in privately own buildings, many of whom were being coerced by landlords into giving up their apartments, subjecting them to intimidation, fear, neglect of the buildings in need of repair, and arson. Delia, when hired, was informed that she, like other reporters, are on call from midnight to 8:00 a.m. in the event they are needed to cover an emergent story.

The night of January 29, at 3:00 a.m., she received a call from the *Dispatch* night desk requesting her to cover a large fire on Second and Clinton Street, Hoboken. She quickly got dressed and woke her father up, asking him to drive her to the fire location, about twelve blocks from their apartment. Twenty minutes after receiving the call, she was heading down Willow Avenue, passing the sites of two major fires, the Eleventh Street and 812 Willow Avenue, wondering what the extent of this new fire would be.

Delia's father dropped her off one block from the fire, where she could see the flames engulfing what seemed like the whole building. The combination of flames and intense smoke ran counter to the chilling winter weather in January. As she got closer to the front part of the building, she could see flames shooting out windows and on through to the roof. She approached deputy chief Joseph Riley, who was standing on the side and asked him if he could brief her on what he knew so far. He said an official statement would be issued in several hours. However, Delia asked him if he could at least let her know if anybody was injured. Riley understood she was doing her job, so he said, "I could tell you this—some tenants at 131 Clinton Street, on the top floor, were trapped and did not get out. We will know more when the fire is completely out, which could take hours."

She asked him, "Do you know how the fire started?"

"Preliminary reports are, it was arson, and it started on the first floor stairwell, ascending up to the top floor, trapping tenants, making it impossible to exit."

She later learned that three tenants had jumped from their windows to escape the fire and one woman was lying on the ground unconscious when the first responders arrived. One mother on the third floor threw her son out the window to a policeman, who caught the four-year-old child. The fire escapes located at the rear of these tenements were engulfed in flames as well, making it impossible to escape. The last comment Riley made was, "After the fire is extinguished, we will have to evaluate its structural integrity before we can remove any of the bodies."

Most of Hoboken's firefighters were present at the fire, requiring the city to rely on support from Jersey City and Union City Fire Department to cover for any other calls for fire service in the city. Present at all major fires in Hoboken and throughout Hudson County was the Red Cross, which was headed by Joseph Leiberwitz, its director. The Red Cross provided hotels and other shelter options to families displaced by fire at their cost. One additional service provided was funeral arrangements and cost of the burials all possible with the generous contribution of others. It was a small comfort to those who lost a loved one but an additional burden that was lifted to grieving families.

By 7:00 a.m., approximately four hours after the first responders arrived at the fire, it was declared extinguished by the Hoboken Fire Department. Structural engineers affiliated with the city entered the three fire-damaged buildings to evaluate its structural integrity for the next part of their role, finding bodies, and the task of removing them. The Hoboken firefighters were no strangers to deadly fires as they started entering each apartment checking for bodies. By 10:00 a.m., it was determined that twenty-one people died in the fire, most of whom were located on the top floor and were children. One family on the top floor seemed to have been huddled together in their last moment of life. The fire had engulfed the top floor, the roof, and fire escapes in the back. In addition, seventeen tenants and six firefighters were treated at the hospital for injuries and smoke inhalation.

Beginning at 10:00 a.m., Delia observed from the sidewalk when the victims' bodies were starting to be removed from the top-floor rear fire escape. They were in body bags being lowered one at a time by a crane, which was brought in to assist with the extraction carefully and respectfully. It was an emotional moment for Delia as tears rolled down her face as she viewed the removal process, and it angered her. Many of the neighbors and onlookers watched this gruesome moment as well. The question in most people's mind was, *Why?* She was no exception. The emotional feeling could not escape her as she was one of the community members affected.

By the afternoon of January 29, Delia was able to write the first of three articles she would submit. The first article provided all the information she had obtained, and a photo of fire protruding from windows at 131 Clinton Street accompanied it as well. Her article identified the twenty-one people who were killed, the firefighters injured, and the fact that thirty families were homeless. It also included an appeal to the public to help the victims by donating to the Red Cross. After submitting her article to Newton for his approval, she went home exhausted and emotionally drained.

The following day, at 9:00 a.m., Delia went to Newton's office requesting a meeting; and Maria arranged for them to meet at 11:00 a.m. Her intention was to share the frustration and ask for guidance on how to deal with all the emotions.

Their meeting started with Delia stating, "Newton, I am very upset with yesterdays' tragedy and feel I should be doing more than just reporting on the fire. I also believe the *Dispatch* has a responsibility to say something in the form of an editorial."

Newton responded, "I know you are very upset about this fire and what's happening with the Hispanic community and feel you have an obligation to represent them. However, you need to remain professional in some way above the fray. I believe the best way you serve this situation is to do your job as a reporter and represent the community with the power of your writing. Remember, as a reporter, you must maintain your integrity and tenacity in seeking the truth."

"What I would like to do is a more comprehensive reporting. Yes, investigative reporting on the fires and gentrification," said Delia.

Newton responded by saying, "Delia, in order for me to approve this effort, you would need to first outline the type of research you would employ, such as who would be interviewed and a timeline to complete the project. You know it would be time-consuming, and I cannot guarantee it would be published. So think about it and get back to me, okay."

"You're right, I am still upset and will give it more thought about how and when I can make an impact. Thanks."

Delia's frustration was reflective of the Hispanic community in general who felt victimized by the system. The deadly fire had taken its greatest toll on them, simply because they occupied tenement housing in Hoboken, which were affordable, all be it rundown and in need of repair. The buildings were replete with violations—absent of fire prevention equipment such as smoke detectors or sprinklers—and the landlords pressured many to vacate their homes. The choice for low-income residents in Hoboken was limited to the Housing Authority projects or Applied Corporation Section 8 housing, both having minimum vacancy. The decline of private sector affordable apartments and the conversion of rental units into condos combined with the fires set the pattern for the population decline especially among the children.

Four days after the fire, the Hoboken fire department, police department, and county prosecutor's office declared that the fire was started by an arsonist with the presence of an accelerant in the stairwell. Witnesses who were driving by around 3:00 a.m. came forward to say they saw two men running out of 131 Clinton Street prior to the fire. The investigation details were articulated by a spokesperson for the prosecutor's office, who confirmed the arson and that they were at a loss for the motive nor did they have a lead on who may have done this. It was stated that the investigation would be ongoing, and the conference closed with an appeal to the public for any information they may have to help in the investigation. It remained unsolved.

This photo shows the aftermath of the fire at 131 Clinton Street, in Hoboken, New Jersey, which killed twenty-one people in January 1979. Courtesy of Hoboken Historical Museum.

CHAPTER 13

Four Fatal Fires

From 1978 to 1980, Delia reported on many fires in Hoboken, with four smaller ones having fatalities. During this period in Hoboken's history, approximately 150 fires occurred throughout the community, affecting hundreds of families and contributing to the gentrification. Seven people died in these fires with most, again, being children. She covered all four fires, writing articles describing the various circumstances for each. All the fires were considered isolated and small compared to the 1973 Eleventh Street fire and the Clinton Street fire, having a combined fatality of thirty-two souls. Delia insisted in her articles that the deceased names be included as well as the landlords. She believed it was the appropriate tribute to the tenants and their families.

Newton supported Delia's inclusion of landlord's names as relevant to the situation. However, many landlords objected to their inclusion, calling it unfair because it implied, they may have culpability. The fact that hundreds of fires had taken place in Hoboken in a relatively short period of time fueled the gentrification and conversion efforts, benefiting the landlords.

March 10, 1978
Housing Authority Fire

On Sunday night, March 12, 1978, Delia reported that the Hoboken Housing Authority, which manages over 1,200 units suffered its worst apartment fire in its history. One tenant was killed in an apartment fire at 560 Marshall Drive. The fire department considered it to be an accidental fire, which started in the kitchen and spread throughout the apartment. The fire department representative stated the fire was contained in the one apartment due to the structural makeup of the building and the rapid response by the department. Delia was able to quote the Housing Authority director, Joseph Caliquire, who extended condolences to the family affected by the fire and assured all the residents that they would be looking at the cause of the fire and take any measures needed to maintain the safety of other tenants. He also reminded the tenants that the Housing Authority buildings were brick structures, making it difficult for fires to spread from apartment to apartment.

May 6, 1978
70 Washington Street

On Saturday afternoon, May 6, 1978, a three alarm fire broke out at 70 Washington Street, a five-story building. It was located directly across from a ShopRite supermarket on Hoboken's main street.

Delia wrote in her article, which appeared in the May 8th edition of the *Dispatch*, that at approximately four thirty, the fire began on the ground floor hallway and quickly traveled up the stairwell, trapping tenants from leaving. Within eight minutes, the fire department arrived to a chaotic scene with tenants hanging from windows, with some on the ground after they had jumped. Panic had set in to the tenants in 70 Washington Street and the two adjacent buildings as fear prevailed. The fire captain at the scene said that some parents dropped their infants from the windows to people below for fear that the children would perish.

Within three hours, the fire department contained the blaze and believed some tenants were not able to survive. The grueling task of going through all the apartments rendered the worst. Two bodies were found charred from the fire. They were later identified as a fifty-year-old mother and her eleven-year-old child who lived on the top floor of the building. Thirty families were left homeless, in addition to the two fatalities. Another ten people were treated at St. Mary's hospital for their injuries. Delia ended her article like the others, requesting donations be processed by the Red Cross whether clothing or funds. The fire was suspected to be arson by the fire department.

October 25, 1979
311 First Street

On October 26, 1979, Delia reported on another fatal fire in Hoboken, which killed two people at 311 First Street, a three-story building. Although it was not considered arson, it did, however, claim the thirty-sixth and thirty-seventh fatal fire victims in the last six years.

Delia, who covered the story, was informed by the fire department spokesman that they had arrived within minutes of the call, but it was too late to save the two. She reported that the mother of four was home with her infant child when the fire ignited her apartment in a short time, killing her and the infant. The other three children fortunately were in school at the time of the afternoon fire. A neighbor described the mother as friendly and helpful to others in the building. A total of four families were displaced by the fire and aided by the Red Cross for temporary accommodations.

The origins of the fire in early afternoon was determined to have been a tragic accident caused by the tenants, resulting in the two deaths and four families being displaced. The landlord who operated a fish store on the ground floor was very sad by the loss of the mother and child, yet he felt fortunate that his business survived the fire, saving his livelihood and those of his employees. He ultimately made a decision not to repair the apartments above his business because he was concerned a future fire could occur, and he had concluded that the business was more financially important than the tenants' rents. To this end, the landlord had the tenant apartments boarded to protect his business.

September 28, 1980
224 Jefferson Street

Another Hoboken tenement fire occurred early on Sunday, September 28, 1980, with two fatalities, an eight-year-old and a two-year-old. Delia was home sleeping when she received the call from the *Dispatch* to cover the fire. When arriving at the site at 6:00 a.m., she was informed that two children had died in the fire. She was also aware that a firehouse was located up the block from 224 Jefferson Street and inquired about the response time. The spokesperson for the fire department indicated that the call for help had been delayed due to the chaos the fire caused. Neighbors were focused on helping the tenants escape the fire and did not call the department. Flames were shooting out of the third-floor apartment where the two children died. Firefighters that were stationed at the neighboring firehouse were exceptionally moved by the tragedy, being so close to their station and knowing they could have saved the children if notified minutes earlier.

The Jefferson Street fire reinforced the fire departments effort to have the city change building codes to include smoke alarms in all tenement buildings. Up to this point, only new construction buildings or extensive renovated buildings were required by code to include smoke detectors and other fire-prevention measures. The department chief wrote another letter to the mayor and city council, urging them to change the fire-prevention codes as per research, which has proven it would save lives. The two children who died represented the thirty-eighth and thirty-ninth fire fatalities since 1973.

Delia's articles covering the fires started to take on a more pointed reporting as she named the casualties and landlords. Prior to the Jefferson Street fire, it did not mention landlords or management. She explained to Newton that she believed it was important to name the landlords and denote whether smoke alarms were present. Community advocates agreed with the fire department that lack of smoke detectors were in fact another neglect contributing to tenants dying. In addition, tenants recognized they were vulnerable when the building they lived in did not have smoke detectors. Some landlords in response to the fire fatalities throughout Hoboken voluntarily installed smoke detectors and secured front entrances, another fire-prevention measure. The city relied on the state inspection of tenement buildings, which occurred every five years, and would issue what was called a green card. Those landlords who were denied an approved inspection could appeal the decision and delay making any upgrades. Delia would end every article on the Hoboken fires with an appeal for donations to the Red Cross, who were present at all major fires in Hoboken, helping victims with temporary housing. Three hundred Hoboken families received assistance from the Red Cross in the last six years.

Hoboken fire kills mother, year-old son

L.D. 10/26/79

By PETER BEGANS

A mother and her year-old son died yesterday afternoon in a two-alarm blaze that seared their apartment above a fish market in Hoboken.

The blaze, which started in a back bedroom where the two were found, was extinguished within 35 minutes, fire officials said. No explanation for the cause of the fire has been given.

The deaths were the first in a Hoboken fire since 21 people died last January in a Clinton Street blaze that was maliciously set, according to officials.

Edna Gadea, 39, and her son, Tawary Colon, who celebrated his first bithday just weeks ago, were found by firemen and carried from the third-floor apartment at 311 First St. Officials said both were declared dead on arrival at St. Mary Hospital.

Rubin Colon, Mrs. Gadea's common law husband and the boy's father, was treated for smoke inhalation and hysteria and released, hospital officials said. Fire Capt. Anthony Mosca, who aided in removing the two bodies from the burning building, was treated for burns of the ears and also released, the hospital said.

Fire officials said the blaze began sometime before 2:40 p.m. One second-floor resident of the building said he did not smell smoke but heard people from upstairs running down and making a lot of commotion.

Truck 2 of Engine Co. 1 was the first vehicle on the scene, according to reports. Firemen said they saw flames rolling out of the rear window. Deputy Chief Edward McDonald said the fireman entered the building with airpacks because of the heavy smoke.

Eyewitnesses said a man named William "Chico" Martinez, who works in a furniture store nearby, climbed up a fire escape on the front of the building and broke a closed window to allow smoke to come out.

Others in the neighborhood helped fireman drag fire hoses through the halls of the building up to the third floor, fire officials said. Two neighborhood men who would not give their names said the smoke in the hallway was too dark to see.

All four families in the building have been relocated because of extensive smoke and water damage to the second and third floors of the building. The Red Cross made arrangements to put all 16 people up at the Meadowlands Motel in North Bergen last night, Red Cross director Joe Lecowitch said.

(Continued on page 5)

A police barricade is set up outside Apicella's fish market in Hoboken, where a two-alarm blaze killed a mother and her infant son in the apartment above the First Street store yesterday afteroon.

Mom, infant killed in blaze

(Continued from page 1)

Two of the families receive Aid to Dependent Children and will be relocated today through the Hudson County Welfare office, sources said.

Mrs. Gadea's surviving children—Lisa, 16, Jasmine, 15, and Francisco, 13—reportedly will be taken in by relatives.

Nilda Alvarado, the woman's sister, said Edna "was a very good woman. She helped everybody."

Fire investigator Capt. Raymond Falco said the fire is still under investigation. Fire officials are scheduled to inspect the building again tomorrow. Falco said he did not know if the structure was in violation of any building or health codes.

Courtesy of the *Hudson Dispatch*

Arson for Profit

To deliberately set fire to a property with the goal to benefit by insurance proceeds and/or another gainful option such as sale of vacant property—a disgraceful business model.

CHAPTER 14

The Markum

Delia's coverage of the Hoboken fires up to this point was mainly on occupied residential housing and the resulting massive displacement of tenants. However, on February 15, 1981, that changed when a commercial building located on Eighth and Madison Street, which was in the process of renovation conversion into a residential building, caught on fire. Previously a five-story toy factory, it was in the process of becoming a fifty-unit loft apartment complex. To convert a commercial building into a loft housing complex was a relatively new concept in Hoboken, whereas in New York City it was prevalent, especially Lower Manhattan. The Applied Corporation also emulated this model by renovating a three-story commercial property on Tenth and Clinton Street into a subsidized apartment building. The city had recently supported the development of affordable moderate-income housing, converting the K&E commercial building. In essence, Hoboken started to pivot away from tenement rehabs to commercial and new upscale construction projects. The era of subsidized rehab tenement buildings had come to an end with the federal government cutbacks.

At approximately midnight, the Hoboken Fire Department dispatch center received calls about a building on Eighth and Madison Street that was on fire. It was mainly ablaze on the top floor and on a lower floor at the back of the building. To the firefighters, it was a model burning strategy used in arson. What was unusual as well, it represented the first time that a condominium building, albeit under construction, was burning in Hoboken. Several fire officials and arson experts were involved in determining its origin. Among the investigators was Leo Guzman, representing the insurance company. Apparently, the insurance company hired him as a consultant to investigate whether it was an intentional fire for insurance fraud. Guzman had developed a reputation for conducting thorough investigations for his clients. He would complete his own evaluations independent of others and compare it to their conclusions. In the Markum case, both Guzman and the fire inspectors agreed it was arson.

Delia's coverage of the fire reminded her of the 1972 Foodtown fire, a nonresidential building, in which arson was concluded and criminal convictions reached. It was also a case Leo Guzman had worked on and helped in the conviction of an arsonist. Her initial article described the Markum as a building bordering a commercial and residential area. She identified the owner as Mr. John Seymore, a Newark attorney, as the developer. A relatively newcomer to the development business, the Markum shows a good promise for success despite the fact Seymore had purchased the building at a high price point. Subsequently, it would surface that he had overpaid and underestimated the cost of renovation. The development consultants did not factor in the environmental abatements required. Seymore had also his own personal financial shortcomings as a result of his compulsive gambling habit. Apparently, these problems led to the misguided remedy: arson and insurance fraud.

Once it was established that the fire's origin was arson, Guzman reached out to his FBI friend, Lester Beene, who had retired recently and hired him as a consultant. He believed Beene would bring the extra perspective needed to solve the case by bringing in his former colleagues at the FBI. The FBI accepted the invitation to investigate arson and insurance fraud. They also knew of Seymore's gambling problems because his name had surfaced in previous gambling cases outside of Newark. Delia, who was not privy about the investigation details, was nevertheless aware that the FBI was involved.

The FBI began their investigation by looking into the background of Markum's ownership, contractors, and employees. This examination brought to light Seymore's business practice in Newark and his gambling involvement with local organized crime businesses where he placed his bets. Secondly, they looked at the developer's list of employees and consultants and discovered that a Michael Mallory had been added as a construction consultant just three months prior to the fire. This rang a bell for them since Mallory was known to the FBI as an arsonist. These factors and the final fire department analysis concluded the fire was, in all probability, arson.

The investigation by the FBI began with them reaching out to Seymore and asking about the role Mallory was playing in the Markum and why was he hired as a construction consultant. Basically, Seymore denied knowing Mallory directly, saying he was recommended by the construction contractor and did not know about his criminal background. Seymore ended his conversation with the agents saying he would have his attorney Mr. Adam Munch reach out to them and follow up on their inquiries. The agents' last comments to Seymore was that they are investigating the fire for arson and fraud, stating that if Mallory cooperated with them on the investigation and if he was involved it would bode well for him.

The following week, Seymore's attorney contacted the FBI officials requesting a meeting. However, they responded that more time was needed on their part as the investigation progressed. This concerned Seymore because he did not know what Mallory would say to the agents and requested his attorney to arrange a meeting as soon as possible. Mr. Munch reached out directly to the Justice Department attorneys, requesting a meeting with the agents, and was scheduled for the following week. In attendance at the meeting were Seymore, Munch, the FBI agents, and an attorney representing the Justice Department. The conversation began with an explanation by the agents that the arson investigation was progressing and the presence of Mallory on the development payroll was suspicious. They also indicated that Seymore's name surfaced in another investigation regarding gambling and loan-sharking operation in Newark. To further complicate the issue, the agent indicated that Seymore's wife was listed as a principal in the Markum and could be implicated should this situation rise to a criminal level. Finally, they stated that their federal taxes were filed jointly, which also could implicate Mrs. Seymore as well. Seymore realized the investigation had progressed significantly concerning his involvement. He requested additional time to consider what had been stated and asked to meet again a week later, giving him more time to consult with his attorney.

Seymore was determined to protect his wife and family from any form of prosecution. He instructed John Munch to speak with the Justice Department attorney, seeking options should he cooperate with the investigation. Munch suggested to them that Seymore may have information regarding the fire and the gambling and loan sharking should he cooperate. Apparently, Seymore had amassed a gambling debt, and he thought of a way in which to pay it off: insurance fraud. Munch suggested that in exchange for Seymore's cooperation, the Justice Department would not implicate Mrs. Seymore in any charges. The DOJ countered the suggestion by insisting that he testify against Mallory and plead guilty to lesser charges. The offer of protected custody was presented to him and his family for their consideration.

A memorandum of cooperation was presented to Seymore and his attorney to consider, but it did require additional consequences affecting him. In exchange for his testimony, his wife would not be implicated and he would have to plead guilty to conspiracy and fraud and receive probation in addition to forfeiting his law license. The insurance company also requested that they get reimbursed for the fire policy paid to Seymore. The indictments were processed separately with Mallory's case severed from Seymore, signaling his cooperation.

Delia had arranged with Newton to cover the stories related to the Markum from the fire to the indictments. She wrote about the fire's uniqueness as the first condominium fire, and secondly, she drew a contrast between this condominium fire from tenement-building fires. Her final article on the Markum was the case's resolution. Eventually, Mallory took a plea deal, which meant Seymore did not have to testify. It required Mallory to plead guilty to arson and conspiracy to commitment fraud but did not have to testify against any other associate. He received a five-year sentence and was required to reimburse the court cost of $3,500.00. Seymore reimbursed the insurance company, sold the Markum, and his family moved from New Jersey to an undisclosed state. Delia's article concluded with the overt comment that the case was resolved as a result of the comprehensive investigation conducted by the FBI.

Righteous Indignation

The act of being angry and disgusted at individuals believing their action was morally reprehensible such as gentrification by fire.

CHAPTER 15

Outrage

The Hoboken fires from 1973 to 1980 had accumulated 39 fatalities; 400 fires; and approximately 3,500 residents displaced, relocating out of the city. In all the fatal fires, which were predominately arson, no one had been held accountable nor arrested. This data mostly affected the Hispanic community, its morale, and it fostered a sense of insecurity. The only relief that existed was the renovation and rental of new apartment buildings by Applied Housing. Although it was becoming more competitive for Applied to acquire properties for renovations, the federal government was still offering Section 8 subsidies, and the city supported the effort.

Three days after the Jefferson Street fire, Delia met with Newton to discuss her idea of the *Dispatch* taking a position on the fires. It was not enough for her to report on the fires, she felt the *Dispatch* had a greater responsibility to the public.

"Newton, I think the public should hear from us in an editorial similarly to the *Jersey Journal* and call out the gentrification impact in Hoboken."

"I agree and will present it to the editorial board for their approval. What else?" asked Newton.

"I would like to write an exposé on the fires and gentrification raising issues, which need to be said."

Newton's response was not exactly what Delia was hoping.

"I don't think it's the right time and could conflict with the editorial."

Delia left Newton's office encouraged with his commitment to pursue an editorial and the fact he did not totally reject her exposé idea.

Although Delia was disappointed, she remained focused on her job assignments and did not give up on her goal of providing an appropriate article about the fires.

The following Friday, Delia asked Maria to joint her for lunch at Biggies Sandwich shop in downtown Hoboken on Madison Street. It was one of their lunchtime spots while attending Hoboken High School.

She and Maria headed for Biggies around twelve noon using Maria's car and doubled-parked in front of the restaurant alongside other patrons' vehicles. Delia saw this as an opportunity to catch up on Maria's young family and her move to Jersey City.

While they were sitting at one of the available tables, a young man came up to them and introduced himself.

"Hi, my name is Vinny Bernardo. Are you the *Dispatch* reporter?"

"Yes," said Delia.

"I'm the manager of buildings cited by you, naming me in the articles you wrote," said Vinny.

Delia sensed in his tone that it was not positive.

"What do you mean?" she responded.

"I manage properties for my uncle who owned two of the properties that burned in Hoboken, and you chose to name him in your articles, and we don't think it was fair."

"Look, I write what I believe to be important facts in an article and naming the landlords is one of them. Nevertheless, we are having lunch now, and it would be better for us if you call my office. Here's my card."

"No, I need to say something now."

By this time, some of the other patrons took notice, especially a police officer who was sitting in a corner table. He walked over and asked if everything was all right.

"Ladies, is everything okay?"

Vinny responded, "I'm just speaking with them about some articles, but it can wait. Thanks, ladies."

Vinny exited Biggies, and the police officer introduced himself.

"My name is Officer Joe Rodriquez. Was I right to intervene?"

"Yes, thank you," said Delia. "We have never met him before, and he came up to us wanting to talk about my work."

"Oh, what work is that?" said Joe.

Maria joined the conversation and stated they worked for the *Dispatch* and Vinny did not like what she wrote. "Oh, by the way, I'm Maria. She is Delia."

"It's a pleasure meeting you, ladies. Enjoy your lunch. Here's my card, should you need anything in the future."

Before Joe walked back to his table, Maria said, "Wait, Delia wants to give you her card, should you need her help."

Delia gave him one of her cards while staring at Maria.

"Thanks," said Joe, accepting her card.

"Maria, I know what you are doing. I'm not interested in meeting anyone new, but rather, we should speak about that creep Vinny," said Delia.

"Yeah, Vinny was a creep, but Officer Joe looked interesting, don't you think, Delia?"

"No comment, just eat your lunch."

After finishing their lunch, they returned to the office and went directly to Newton's office.

"What's up, ladies?" asked Newton.

Delia proceeded to explain that they went to lunch and some guy named Vinny came up to them complaining about the articles she wrote naming the landlords.

"Well, get used to it. Some people like what you write, and others don't. It comes with the territory. What counts is writing the truth. However, you need to be careful anyway, although there is no need to worry."

"Thanks," said Delia as they left Newton's office.

*****

What Delia and Maria didn't know was that Vinny's uncle, Mike Gusto, owned twelve tenement apartments in Hoboken under an LLC (limited liability corporation), and three had been involved with fires. The state records showed Michael Gusto as the sole principal owner. He was also a business owner operating a local bar called the Wharf

Tavern. It was frequented by locals, known to facilitate illegal sports wagering and numbers betting. The fact was that Gusto owned the tenement properties with silent partners from his circle of friends. Vinny, also known as Skinny Vinny, managed the properties for his uncle, mainly collecting rents, renting units, and supervising repairs.

Vinny who grew up in Hoboken was a high-school dropout who got involved with the drug scene and had been arrested as a teenager several times for use and distribution of drugs. Now thirty years old, his steady income came from managing the properties and assisting his uncle in the tavern.

A week prior to Vinny confronting Delia and Maria at Biggies, his uncle called him in to speak about the fire articles that named him as the principal owner. He wanted Vinny to address it.

"Look, I want you to contact these people from the newspaper and let them know to stop naming us," said Gusto to Vinny.

"What do you want me to do?"

"I'm telling you get them to stop. Some of our guys don't like the attention. These articles suggest we are involved with the fires and could bring undue scrutiny by law enforcement. Understand?"

Gusto was Vinny's maternal uncle and served as a surrogate father to help his sister with her single parenting. He knew of Vinny's drug use arrest in the past and warned him not to bring drugs in the business.

Often critical of his work ethics, Gusto told him, "Vinny, don't screw this up, okay?"

Obviously, the approach he used a week later at Biggies was not exactly smart and effective. This intimidation tactic would not work on Delia, and she made it clear to him that the *Dispatch* would continue to name the landlords in all future articles related to fires in Hoboken.

Vinny continued to be pressured by his uncle to stop the landlord naming but did not know what to do.

The following day, while Delia was writing her next article, she received a call from Joe Rodriquez.

"Hello, Delia, this is Joe Rodriquez. I'm just following up to see how you're doing after yesterday's encounter."

"Joe, thank you for calling. I'm doing fine. I spoke with my editor who reminded me it's part of our challenge as a reporter. How are you doing, Joe?" said Delia.

"I'm doing terrific, and that's also why I'm calling to ask you if you would like to have dinner with me."

"Ah, so it was not just a follow-up, was it?" asked Delia. "I also didn't think Biggies was a spot to pick up dates."

"How about dinner?" repeated Joe.

"Yes, when?" responded Delia.

"Saturday is a perfect day, and 7:00 p.m. a perfect time, okay. Where can I pick you up?"

"Not at Biggies, but rather at 1207 Willow Avenue apartment 22R," said Delia. "One thing, where are we going, and any special dress requirement?"

"Let's go to a place I know in Manhattan called Sofrito. It has Spanish food and Latin music. You do know how to dance salsa and meringue, don't you?" said Joe.

"Absolutely, I look forward to dinner as well. See you at 7:00 p.m. Saturday," said Delia as she hung up.

Delia was smitten by Joe's charm and his respect for her work. Their Saturday date went well and developed into a close friendship.

CHAPTER 16

Vinny

Delia had put her encounter with Vinny behind her and chalked it up as a passage for a new reporter to experience. Her perspective of writing the truth for public good does not always sit well with all, another lesson to be learned.

In the fall of 1980, Hoboken continued to experience fires, most absent of fatalities, but they contributed to gentrification of low- and moderate-income families. Rents and homeownership costs were gradually on the rise while affordable housing availability declined. On the national political scene dominating the news, fifty US government workers assigned to Iran were taken hostage by college students and political operatives protesting the US support of its ousted leader Mohammad Reza Shah of Iran. The hostage takers demanded the return of the Shah in exchange for the Americans held captive. The Iranians motive was to try the Shah as a traitor to their people and recover the financial gains he took with him. This issue, combined with a rampant inflation rate, played a major role in the 1980 presidential election.

The incumbent president Jimmy Carter was being challenged by former governor of California Ronald Reagan, who was also a former Hollywood actor. The November election for president of the United States drew many policies contrast on domestic and foreign issues. Reagan projected himself as a fiscal conservative advocating for cutbacks in domestic programs across the board, lowering taxes, and enhancing a market-driven economy. The Iran-hostage saga proved too difficult an issue to overcome for President Carter, who had attempted to resolve it diplomatically and a failed military rescue. Governor Reagan went on to defeat President Carter in the November election while the hostages remained confined. Finally, days prior to the inauguration of the new president, President Carter was able to free the hostages through diplomacy, the final accomplishment in his administration.

But for the fires, the city of Hoboken had attempted to strike a balance between affordable housing and the newer developments by supporting the Section 8 units developed by the Applied Corporation and other smaller entities. However, the Section 8 subsidies would be severely cut back by the new administration. President Reagan held to his policy position as a fiscal conservative cutting social programs and housing subsidies. The federal housing budgetary cuts proved to be pivotal in Hoboken's gentrification by reducing the support for new affordable housing units. The Applied Company relied on the federal Section 8 subsidies to acquire tenements and renovate apartments for low- and moderate-income families. They were able to continue the development of affordable units for only two more years, utilizing the carryover subsidies committed under the Carter administration before virtually ending their role providing affordable housing.

Reporting of the continuous Hoboken fires at the *Dispatch* was relegated to Delia. In her writings, she tried to include the humane side of the tragedies of fatalities or gentrification alone. The displacement of families and the victims were egregious acts when arson for profit is the impetus. She wondered how landlords could condone arson and when would it end. The city of Hoboken's effort under Mayor Cappiello was not one of urgency, attributing the fires to the low-income residents, personal disputes, and neglect. Yet the installation of smoke detectors were optional for landlords, according to city code. The advocacy for smoke detectors was undertaken by the fire department that had the responsibility to fight the fires and remove the bodies of the deceased.

On April 12, 1981, yet another fire occurred in a row of tenement buildings at 60–64 Washington Street, a block away from city hall. One of the four buildings was owned by Jefferson LLC and managed by Vinny. This coincidence was not surprising to Delia, who knew she would write up the article and include Gasto and Vinny's names. The fire managed to displace twenty families, again mainly of Hispanic background. The Hoboken rental market at this point was out of reach financially for the low- and moderate-income families that made up the displaced, leading them to move out of Hoboken. Delia noted in her article "the families lost their apartments, possessions and the community they called home."

A week after Delia wrote the articles on the 60–64 Washington Street fires, she asked Maria, who was pregnant at the time, to join her for lunch at Benny Tudino's pizzeria, another lunch spot they frequented while in high school. They both were fans of the largest and most delicious slice of pizza served in Hoboken, only at Benny Tudino's. Maria found a parking space a block from Benny's, and as they were walking toward the restaurant, Delia spotted a guy across the street who seemed to be staring at them. She finally recognized him to be Vinny. As she and Maria entered Benny's, Delia looked back and saw he had stopped directly across the street. Upon entering the restaurant, they ordered three slices to share one and a half each and sat at one of the tables. Delia was upset about seeing Vinny, who she believed was stalking them.

She told Maria, "I'm calling Joe," and went to the pay phone. Since she knew he was on duty, Delia called the police desk and requested to speak with Officer Joe Rodriquez. Upon reaching him, she asked for him to pass by Benny's because Vinny seemed to be stalking her and Maria, possibly waiting for them outside.

Joe stopped by Benny's within five minutes of receiving the call but not in an emergency mode. He entered Benny's and went straight for Delia's table.

"Hi, ladies, I got here as soon as possible. I looked around the block but did not see Vinny. Are you guys sure it was him?"

"Absolutely," said Delia, and Maria confirmed it. "He was across the street."

"Okay, but without him being present outside, I can't do much other than write a report. Should this happen again, then we will be able to take some action. I know that might be disappointing, but legally, I am limited. Don't be mad at me, Delia, okay?"

"Mad, how can I be mad, you're paying for the pizzas."

"Now I know why you called me. Just kidding. I believed you and will write that report to be filed."

That evening Delia was home with her parents. She was watching TV when, at about 8:30 p.m., she heard a loud banging at her door. It seemed like an unusual knock, and she asked who it was before opening the door. There was no response. Nevertheless, she opened it and was surprised to see what was lying on the floor. A copy of the *Dispatch* newspaper was lying on the floor with a sharp stick protruding through it. It was partially covered with what appeared to be ketchup designed to look like blood. Obviously, it was a message to her and a form of intimidation.

Delia immediately called the police and Joe, who had completed his shift and had taken the call from home. Both the police and Joe arrived within ten minutes to find the newspaper still in the same place she found it. She had not touched the item on the floor and asked the police to remove it. Joe immediately knew who would be responsible for this act and informed the police officer. However, again, Joe admitted that absent someone witnessing who left the newspaper, it would be difficult for a resolution. However, after the police removed the item and took Delia's statement, they assured her and her parents a report would be filed. Joe told Delia he would speak with his captain tomorrow to see what action can be taken.

The next morning Joe went to Captain O'Riely's office to talk about Delia's encounters with Vinny hoping to get some direction. Captain O'Riely said he knew who Vinny was and knew his uncle Gusto. He believed that Joe should not be directly involved in the issue given his relationship with Delia. Joe was very upset about what had happened the evening before and expressed his anger toward Vinny. He stressed what Delia and her parents experienced after seeing what he called a threat. The captain understood his feelings on the issue and explained the lack of evidence to accuse Vinny formally. He did, however, say something has to be done.

Captain O'Riely decided to call Detective Lombardo to his office with the idea of him taking the lead on this case. The detective entered O'Riely's office with Joe present. They relayed the situation and showed him the tainted newspaper.

"Detective, this situation is one that may lack direct evidence that Vinny was behind it, but I think you know him and his uncle. They had expressed displeasure about articles written by Ms. Delgado for the *Dispatch*. Tomorrow, I want you to visit Vinny at his house and let him know we believe he is behind the prank that can elevate to a criminal act. Let him know to end it or we will continue to pursue it with his uncle," said the captain.

"I got it, Captain. It will be taken care of tomorrow," responded Detective Lombardo.

The captain reiterated to Joe not to get involved, that the detective will handle it, then he ended the meeting.

The next day, at 8:00 a.m., Detective Lombardo went to visit Vinny at his tenement apartment on Adams Street, which he shared with his mother, Rose.

He knocked on his door, and Rose opened the door. She was surprised to see Lombardo, who she knew from the neighborhood.

"Detective, good morning. What can I do for you?" said Rose.

"Hi, Mrs. Bernardo, I'm here to see Vinny. Is he home?"

"Yes, but he's sleeping."

"Please wake him up, I need to speak with him," said Lombardo.

"I hope he's not in trouble," said Rose.

"That's the point of speaking to him. I want to avoid trouble."

"I'll go wake him. He will be right out."

Two minutes after Vinny's mother went to get him, Vinny came out from behind a closed curtain leading to his room.

"Vinny, do you know who I am?" said Lombardo. "You should. I arrested you years ago on drug possession."

"Oh yeah, I remember. What can I do for you?"

"Look, Vinny, I'm here because we received a complaint from the *Hudson Dispatch* newspaper that you may be harassing one of their reporters, Ms. Delgado. Now I'm not saying you're the one, but I am saying, if you are, end it. This could lead to criminal charges if you are involved, understand? I just want to avoid problems for you and your uncle, so stay away from that reporter."

"I don't know what you are talking about detective," said Vinny.

"Good, then leave it that way. Stay away. Rose, sorry to have bothered you. Thanks. Take care, Vinny," said Lombardo as he left the apartment.

The door closed behind him, and he could hear Rose yelling at Vinny, "What the hell did you do? Is this your uncle's doing?"

"No, Ma, I'm not involved."

By days end, Vinny's uncle Gasto had heard that some law enforcement figure had gone to his nephew's house. Gasto's friends had called him at the business and said they believed an FBI agent had gone to see Vinny about the fires, which was false. Gusto was very upset to hear about this and wanted to speak with Vinny to find out the truth. He arranged for one of his tavern workers to locate Vinny and bring him back to the business.

When Vinny arrived at the establishment, he could tell his uncle was in a bad mood by his expression.

"Get in here, Vinny," said Gusto. "What the hell is going on?"

"Oh, you must have gotten word that someone came to see me this morning. It was Detective Lombardo, the guy that lives up the block from me."

"Detective Lombardo? The word on the street was that an FBI had visited with you."

"No, Uncle Gasto. It was Lombardo, I swear it."

"Regardless of who it is, it's not good to be seen talking to a cop. What did he want?" said Gasto.

"He was asking me to stop harassing the *Dispatch* reporter who wrote the articles about the fires naming us."

"The *Dispatch* reporter? What did you do?"

"I was just trying to scare her so she would stop writing the articles with our names."

"Who told you to do that?"

Vinny looked puzzled and said, "You did."

"Boy, you are a real *stunod*. I never told you to harass anyone, especially a reporter. In fact, I think you're losing it, Vinny, and I also think you're back on drugs again. I want you to lie low for a week, understand?" said Uncle Gusto.

"I will," said Vinny as he left the tavern.

That same morning Delia met Newton and informed him about the threat she experienced. She told him a police report had been filed and Joe was meeting with his captain to see if anything further would come of it. While they were still speaking in Newton's office, Joe walked in and informed them of his meeting with the captain, who assigned a detective. Newton was appreciative of Joe's effort on behalf of Delia and thanked him for his help. Joe mentioned that should anything develop on this situation, he would keep them informed.

Newton turned to Delia and asked if she was okay.

She said, "Yes, of course."

"Good, you're doing a great job," said Newton.

On July 4, 1980, Delia heard good news. Maria gave birth to her second child, August Luis, the new younger brother of his sister, Carmen. Maria asked Delia to serve as August's godmother along with Danny Bonet, her brother-in-law, who would be the godfather. August was baptized at St. Joseph's Church, Hoboken, where Father Joseph presided over the baptismal ceremony.

Delia arranged to use the church hall for a small reception after the service. The family and friends gathered for a fun time with food, drinks, and Latin music. The event also included conversation about the fires and how about half the people present at the baptism who had lived in Hoboken no longer resided in the mile-square city.

CHAPTER 17

The Proposal

Delia's role as a reporter for the *Hudson Dispatch* placed her in the unique situation of her career responsibility and her struggle to understand her role as a Hobokenite of Puerto Rican background. She had successfully completed her college degree from UMASS; interned at a major nationally recognized newspaper the *Boston Globe*; served as a reporter for the *New-York Mirror* newspaper; and now found herself as a local reporter during a dark historic period in her hometown, Hoboken. She understood the responsibility as a professional but also accepted her role as a community member. This helps Delia define what was missing in the dialogue of Hoboken's dilemma of fires, gentrification, and fatalities. She also knew that a segment of the community was indifferent to the problems that targeted low-income tenants and not them.

The fact-finding effort Delia undertook to support the exposé article included examining the cause and effect of the Hoboken fires. She originally set out to obtain an official document compiled by the city that would combine the various components describing the fires of the 1970s. However, what she found was that it did not exist, nor was there interest in completing one on the part of the city. She inquired with the Community Development Agency, mayor's office, and public library archives to no avail. A report summarizing the fires and the city's effort to address them was never compiled. She concluded the city officials preferred not talking about it, let alone documenting the dark side of the renaissance.

Delia realized that a document of this nature could be written but required a dedicated researcher to examine the various fire reports, news coverage, law enforcement investigations, and other city agencies related to the consequences, which was a daunting task. She accepted the fact that it was too time-consuming for her to undertake, but it was a new challenge for her to identify a person and funding to chronicle this historic period. Her next move was to ask for a meeting with Newton for his input, seeking advice on how to proceed.

The following Monday, Newton met with Delia, describing her quest to obtain a copy of the nonexisting report. She explained to him how other communities would document historic events to contribute to literature and closure. She asked Newton for his thoughts on her new challenge and hopefully his recommendation.

"Delia," said Newton, "I can't believe you are looking to take on another project, yet you have not completed the exposé."

"I know, but I did not seek out to create a new project because I really thought a report existed and was completed by one of the city's agencies. As for the exposé, that draft is almost completed and will be ready next week."

"So how do you propose this new project can proceed? Who would pay for it and be responsible to complete? Quite frankly, you're talking about a book on the Hoboken fires. Why don't you consider writing it yourself?"

"I never thought of it that way, and am not inclined to take up the task."

"Okay, what I think you should do is define exactly what you are looking for in a report of this nature. Secondly, you need to write the objective into a proposed project capable of receiving funding from a private or governmental entity. Getting back to the book, this would be a good segue for you to write the book. You're the right person to do it."

"I believe your idea of writing a grant is a promising strategy and will get started on this task, of course outside of my responsibility as a reporter. I will first identify funding sources and their requirement by researching it at the library."

Delia left Newton's office and realized she took on yet another major task.

Delia spent time at the Hoboken Public Library researching various philanthropic sources that could fund the project. One private grant entity stood out. It was called the Parra-Martinez Foundation, located in Manhattan, New York. Its mission is to provide funding to Latino-based programs promoting education, social justice, and public information grants. The foundation's main funding is from a group of hedge fund managers working out of Wall Street. What drew her to this funding entity was the fact it had previously provided seed money to a Bronx nonprofit that undertook a similar project as the one proposed by Delia examining the 1970s impact of gentrification and fires in the Bronx. Delia identified the requirements for the foundation and saw that a phone number was provided to assist those who would pursue funding. She called the foundation the next day and asked to schedule a meeting with their funding counselor. She obtained an appointment for the following Monday and requested the afternoon off from the *Dispatch* to attend the meeting.

At the foundation meeting, Delia met Mr. Donald Foster, who represented the Parra-Martinez Foundation. He greeted Delia warmly.

"Ms. Delgado, please come in. Have a seat. Thank you for calling the other day and explaining your interest in the foundation."

"Thank you for meeting with me. As I stated over the phone, I am presently a reporter for the *Hudson Dispatch* but am here as a private citizen."

"I understand. Didn't you work at one time at the *New York Mirror* covering the Bronx?"

"Yes, about three years ago, right before they closed. That's where I had heard about your foundation."

"Very good. Let's jump into the foundation funding options and how an application is considered. First, let me provide you with one of our brochures describing our goals, objectives and identifies areas we fund. You should know that most of our past awards went to projects in New York City. However, we have funded grants outside of New York as well."

"Great, that was one of my concerns."

"Delia, the problems you have described in Hoboken, I believe, is worthy for the consideration by the foundation committee for its merit. Your proposal must meet the criteria set out by our guidelines and clearly provide the social justice impact on the community. I am going to give you a funding packet which outlines the process and application forms to be completed. It has several components. First, the proposal needs to identify the social justice issue affecting the community, and secondly, the overall objective of the project basically answering why you would seek funding. A budget page outline is provided in the packet and finally the process you would use to identify personnel funded by the grant. I know it sounds difficult, but the instructions are meant to help. You also know you can call me if you have any questions. Delia, I have one more question for you. Will you be included in the grant as a funded person?"

"At this point, I don't have any intension to be funded by the grant, but rather, I will serve as a pro bono consultant."

"Very good. You have your charge, Delia. Good luck."

"Thank you, Mr. Foster," said Delia. Then she left his office and returned to Hoboken.

The funding application as Mr. Foster had described was divided into three components. She was determined to complete the application and submit it as soon as possible since the next funding quarter was approaching in six weeks. Delia began the application by writing about the fatal fires that impacted mainly Hispanic low-income tenants. In addition, the gentrification of families created an exodus of thousands from Hoboken. Her goal was to research and compile a document that can serve as a summary of the 1970s fires. Its further objective was to provide the community of Hoboken with a historic document, the Puerto Rican community with closure, and a sociological research paper contributing to the academic community.

Delia believed this document should be completed by an academic or a professional planner. The incorporation of fire reports, demographic trend documents, Hoboken economic patterns, and the Puerto Rican diaspora dynamic would need to be included. She proposed that the grant would fund a lead researcher and clerical staff expenditure, and a nonpaid community advisory board would assist in the project. Delia, as the application point person, would serve on the board and recruit the other members of the board. The board would include a tenant advocate, displaced family representative, city official identified by the mayor, and herself. A budget page was developed based on the proposal outline for $ 25,000.00. The budget covered the cost of two personnel members, supplies, advertising cost, and printing. She also identified an in-kind contribution of office space provided by Mr. Garcia's nonprofit and Delia nonpaid consultant effort. It was anticipated that the project would be completed in a six-month period and would include a public presentation.

Within three weeks of meeting with Mr. Foster, Delia completed the application and submitted it to the foundation for consideration. Mr. Foster indicated the foundation board was scheduled to meet within a month and inform her of their decision immediately thereafter.

A month and a half had passed since she submitted the proposal when she heard from the foundation that the proposal was not accepted for funding. The foundation board applauded the application, which was well-written and did have merit. However, they rejected the proposal for funding because they believed the city of Hoboken should underwrite this project and not abdicate their responsibility. Mr. Foster contacted Delia explaining the board's decision and encouraged her to pursue other funding sources.

Delia was disappointed by the decision but was not discouraged as she refocused on the exposé. In addition, the fires were occurring almost daily, keeping her busy as she covered them for the *Dispatch*.

Hoboken: A Tale of Two Cities

Delia viewed the gentrification by fire in her beloved Hoboken as tragic, unfair, and counter to her sense of decency. She also recognized that the changes also brought needed improvements to housing and the quality of life. As a student of communication studies, she learned how poetry and literature provides us all an in-depth perception of reality. A common literary term used by many describing Hoboken's diverse community is "Hoboken: A Tale of Two Cities." This thought took her back to its literary reference.

In 1859, Charles Dickens, a novelist and social critic, wrote the saga *A Tale of Two Cities* about the French Revolution, which took place in the late 1700s. Yet the opening lines of his book resonated to Delia relating it to the Hoboken fires. Dickens describes the economic divisions and tragedies of the times in France. On a smaller scale yet in a relevant way, Delia sees the Hoboken fires fit into his prose.

> It was the best time, it was the worst of times, it was the age of wisdom, it was the epoch of belief, it was the epoch of incredulity, it was the season of darkness. It was the spring of hope, it was the winter of despair. (Charles Dickens)

CHAPTER 18

Continuous Conflagration

During the summer months of 1981, Hoboken was in a state of alert, given the many fires throughout the community. The fire department described their role as fighting one continuous fire throughout the city. Residents of tenement apartments were on edge, fearing their building could be next and, ultimately, fearing for their lives. Delia wrote in her latest article, "To live in peace should be every one's goal in life, but peace does not co-exist with fear." Many families accommodated their landlords to vacate because they feared arson and they chose to protect their family. The group of newly relocated families was never calculated in the displacement total attributed to gentrification. Yet hundreds of families moved out of Hoboken from 1977 to 1981, reducing the overall Hispanic families and replacing them with higher-income bracket, many of which were singles. Multibedroom units, which previously housed families with children, were now being rented to roommates at a higher rent. Delia believed that the changing demographics trend of Hoboken is irreversible and driven by greed.

Ernest Hemingway once wrote, "Courage is grace under pressure," a trait shown by tenants who faced the potential of tragedy. Many tenants had very little option but to stay the course hoping the fires would end. During the fires, heroic acts and unflinching commitment to save lives were undertaken by neighbors, firefighters, and policemen. But the courage to face a fire while it's still burning and act heroically happened on July 30, 1981, to a fourteen-year-old girl, India Montes.

Delia covered the July 30 fire at 165 Third Street and was most impressed to learn of India Montes's heroic act that evening. It prompted her to write the article focused on India's action to save her neighbors. Delia wrote that while walking home from a friend's house late July 30, India saw that a fire was raging in front of 165 Third Street, a four-story tenement building. She summoned her courage to run into the building and knock on all the tenants' doors, alerting them of the fire. The fire, which was started in the garbage cans located by the main entrance, was poised to engulf the building. What was also amazing was that she pulled the fire alarm located on the corner before sprinting into the building. India Montes saved lives the evening of July 30.

The following day, Delia received a call at the end of her day and was very surprised to hear Vinny on the line.

"Ms. Delgado, this is Vinny Bernardo, and I would like to speak with you for a moment."

Delia, thinking she needed to remain professional but still angry at him, said, "Look, I really shouldn't be talking to you after what you did to me and my family."

"I know, but that's why I called," said Vinny.

"All right, what do you want, Vinny?"

"First, I want to apologize for my action, and I don't blame you if you're still angry. I have joined NA, Narcotics Anonymous, a newly formed group in Hoboken designed to help former drug users. They have given me a new perspective in life, and that's why I called."

"Vinny, if you are sincere about this change and apology, I hold no grudges. But you know I take the tragic fires in Hoboken to heart, and I think you may have important information on this issue. Would you be willing to speak about the fires?"

"Ms. Delgado, I work for my uncle and his partners, so I can't speak on the record about the fires. Maybe someday," said Vinny.

"I understand. However, if you do decide to speak, promise me, you'll call me first, okay?" said Delia.

"You are truly a dedicated reporter," said Vinny, then he hung up the phone.

At midday, on Friday, August 14, Delia was at her desk thinking about her two-week vacation starting at the end of her workday. She had planned with Joe to take several day trips to museums and the Jersey shore and spend time with her mother who was not feeling well.

At 1:30 p.m., Newton called Delia asking her to meet in his office. Delia proceeded to his office and was surprised to see Joe present as well. Newton asked her and Maria to sit down.

Delia said, "What's going on?"

"Ladies I have been informed by Joe and Captain O'Riely that early this morning a body was found in the

Hoboken cove on Fourteenth Street. It has been prelimi-
narily identified as one Vincent Bernardo."

"Oh no, I spoke with him two weeks ago on the phone.
He had told me about getting his act together and not using
drugs anymore," said Delia with stress in her voice.

Joe added, "The department and county prosecutor's
office is investigating the case because it does look like a
homicide. They are looking to see if it was drug related or
another reason. Time will tell. You just need to know that
you did not have anything to do with it."

Both Delia and Maria left Newton's office quietly and
went to compose themselves in the lady's room. Newton
asked Joe to take Delia home and make sure she relaxes
during vacation, forgetting about her job. Although Delia
was sad to hear about Vinny's demise, she also believed that
the truth about the fatal fires might have died with Vinny.

During her two-week vacation period, Delia had the
opportunity to discuss her plan with her parents to leave
the *Dispatch*. She envisioned staying long enough to complete the exposé she clamored writing about Hoboken's fatal
fires and gentrification. Her parents were supportive of her
plan and shared their own vision as well. Apparently, Juan
and Elba were looking into retiring and hoping they could
move to Orlando, Florida, where both had family members
living there. The Orlando area was becoming an enclave
of the Puerto Rican community much like Hoboken was
in the sixties. Delia was not expecting to hear that from
her parents but knew it would be a good move for them.
Her father told her he could arrange for the apartment to
be transferred into her name or a one-bedroom apartment

could be facilitated. It would mean Delia paying rent, but at a subsidized rate. The fact that her parents did not pay rent because Juan worked for the Applied Corporation allowed them to save sufficient funds to buy a home in Orlando. Ironically, in retirement, they would buy their first home.

Delia's tenure at the *Dispatch* was originally planned for a short period of time until she could obtain a more attractive job in a larger newspaper. She envisioned her presence in the New York media scene and not three years later still serving the community of Hoboken. The fires in Hoboken however were too compelling for her to leave at this time, but she knew a change was needed on her part. She had spoken to Newton about the exposé but had not followed up with the proposed outline he had requested. However, Delia was ready for the task, given the continuing fires, and informed Newton it would be submitted for his approval.

*****

On Monday, October 12, 1981, Columbus Day, a fire at 65 Park Avenue claimed the lives of two children ages two and seven. The fire department arrived at the fire to find it engulfed with flames and the tenants in a panic. Apparently, a piece of furniture was set ablaze in the second-floor hallway, which ignited the five-story building, trapping the tenants above the second floor. The two children, who lived on the top floor, were separated from their mother in the chaos and lost their lives as they huddled together, comforting each other in their last moments. Delia's coverage of this fire was heartbreaking to her.

"Yet another fire claiming innocent children," she wrote. "Identified as arson with no resolution in sight."

Two weeks after the 65–67 Park Avenue fire that claimed the life of two children, a new fatal fire occurred on October 25, 1981, at the corner of Twelfth and Washington Street. Also identified as arson related, eleven people were killed by this raging fire and displacing fourteen families. The fire department's initial investigation found bottles of gasoline in the stairwell area, moving the flames upward to the top floor. The majority of those killed were of the same family located on the top floor. It was reported that a conflict had occurred between the tenants and landlord who wanted the building vacant. This may have contributed to the fire. The building was sold three months after the fire. It was delivered vacant.

Three weeks after the Twelfth Street fire, Delia heard, through her contacts in the community, that several tenant groups were planning a demonstration for Saturday, November 14. She informed Newton of the pending event and requested to cover the story along with a photographer. Newton agreed with her and assigned Piere Magno, *The Dispatch* photographer, to support her coverage. On the day of the demonstration, she met Piere late morning on Twelfth and Washington Street where the event would start, marching toward city hall.

The following Monday, Delia's article focused on the continuation of fires, displacement of tenants, and the overall gentrification, prompting the resistance from local tenant rights group. Marchers were comprised of tenants, clergy, and Hispanic business owners. The Hispanic business owners had met with the mayor in the past, requesting the city take a more proactive position on the fires. The mayor, a former policeman, believed the responsibility for arson investigation rested mainly on the county prosecutor's office.

On Saturday, November 14, a rally and peaceful demonstration gathered in front of the Twelfth Street fire site with 150 people initially. However, it turned into a march that traversed through neighborhoods with tenement buildings growing to four hundred by the time they arrived at city hall. They chanted, "Stop the war on the poor" and "Stop arson for profit." Some marchers carried homemade signs with names of victims who died in the fires, and one sign read, "The price of renaissance: evictions and homelessness." Several leaders of the march spoke in front of city hall and expressed their anger and frustration toward the mayor for not taking a stronger position against the fires. The demonstration was well received by residents of poor neighborhoods they marched through but received a cold nonreactive response from other community members. The divide was viewed by many as economic disparity, political, and racial. The political overtone was evident with the marchers and the Hispanic community, but it did not have an impact on the incumbent mayor, as six months later, he was reelected in a landslide and virtually unopposed. This was evidence to Delia that the political will to address the fires and gentrification was not shared by the Hoboken democratic machine and the community at large.

Fire victims who were displaced found themselves homeless with only a few of the low-and moderate-income families remaining in Hoboken because they were able to be placed in the limited affordable apartments available in the Housing Authority or Applied Corporation. The city's only additional available units were three aged hotels, which basically housed singles but, through the city's effort, accommodated small families displaced by the fires. Two of these hotels, the American and the Pinter housed some of these families but were also subjected to the real estate developers' pressures to sell.

On November 21, the American Hotel located on the corner of River Street and Hudson Place directly across from the PATH station, claimed two lives in an early morning fire. It was only five weeks after the Twelfth Street fire when this new tragedy occurred, displacing all its tenants. Among the displaced families were two residents that had been homeless due to a previous tenement fire. The fire represented one less location in Hoboken that was used to help displaced victims.

Delia wrote the article covering the fire, describing it as an additional strike against Hoboken's low- and moderate-income families, asking how this ordeal could continue to befall on them especially the Hispanic community. She never believed it could get worse or that more fatalities related to gentrification by arson were still possible. The American Hotel was sold and redeveloped into commercial units.

Hudson Dispatch, Monday November 16, 1981

Marchers Against Arson for Profit clog traffic on 14th Street in Hoboken Saturday.

Photo by Ted Boswe

400 march for Hoboken's poor

By ROY KAHN
Staff Writer

HOBOKEN— The fears and problems tied to being poor in this city were dramatized this weekend as more than 400 protesters marched against arson for profit and what they called "the war against the poor."

The peaceful demonstration began at noon on Saturday and, starting at 12th and Washington streets where 11 people died in a fire police said was set, wound its way through the more-impoverished sections of the city.

Along the route, banner-toting marchers chanted, "Stop the war against the poor," and "We demand rent control, stop the arson now," as they urged bystanders to join them.

By the time the marchers reached City Hall, their number had doubled, and the procession stretched for three blocks.

The demonstration had been sparked by the deaths of 11 persons last month in two tenement fires police believe were set.

At the rally which followed, it was clear the theme included a call for political change as well as an end to "arson for profit."

Organizers argued that there is a link between the city's vacancy decontrol law adopted July 15 and cases of tenant harassment.

The law permits owners to increase rents on vacated apartments by 25 percent, more than five times the increase allowed under the previous rent control law.

Tom Soto, a leader of the New Jersey All Peoples Congress, told the demonstrators at City Hall that there is a "war between the poor and the rich." He charged that Mayor Steve Cappiello and the City Council are working with "the real estate companies and the banks" to force the poor out of the city.

Expressing a sentiment voiced by many other speakers, he added, "We have to get the mayor to get the local government out, and replace them with people who answer our needs."

While march organizer Juan Garcia, executive director of Citizens United for New Action contended the march was not political, many speakers directed their attacks at Cappiello.

Garcia drew boos from the crowd when he read a 2-year-old newspaper clipping in which Cappiello was quoted as saying the poor generate more rubbish than others, also charging that sanitary standards are not as strict in Puerto Rico as they are in the United States.

For the marchers and organizers, the demonstration was a successful end to two weeks of planning. It was the first time a coalition of tenant groups, not only from Hoboken but from other parts of New Jersey as well as New York, rallied to demonstrate their concern for the problems of Hoboken's poor. These problems include increasing rents and a dwindling supply of apartments for low-income residents.

"We have to do something, we can't let ourselves go down," said 15-year-old Diego Castellanos. "I think we can influence the City Council ... just watch."

But getting the message to the community could be a bit more difficult. For while the demonstrators were cheered on Willow and Jackson streets, they were met with a stony silence by the shoppers on Washington Street.

See MARCH, Page 14

Befallen

Dark times we face smoke filled it seems
Trapped in our mind of nature's wrath
Why must it be so sad and melancholy
We strive like others to reach our station
  in life
But times have befallen on truth we see
However sure as gold the spirit does rise
  not a surprise
Rising in time stronger yet filled with
  query
Seeking peace and justice in closure our
  hearts longs
Memory is forever healing in our soul,
  minds, and hearts

CHAPTER 19

The Research

Planning the expose was important to Delia, and getting it right was necessary for achieving her goal. The outline she would present to Newton would have to be cogent and structured in a way to collect the needed data. She knew the mayor, code official, fire department, and police department representatives had to be on the interview list. In addition, the county prosecutor, the FBI, tenant advocates, and displaced families would be interviewed. The outline was prefaced with her reviewing all the articles written about the fires and Hoboken's gentrification.

Delia arranged to meet with Newton the first week in December to review the outline she had forwarded to him prior to their meeting for his consideration. The meeting with Newton started with him acknowledging the outline and thanking her for preparing it. He expressed his support for the outline and requested to add items he thought necessary.

"It's a good outline. However, I need a timeline, starting with review of past articles. I agree you need to read articles from *Jersey Journal*, *Hudson Dispatch*, and the *New*

York Times. However, I think you should also look up a fire which occurred in 1972 at a Foodtown store on Third and Jackson Street. Although commercial property, nevertheless, it was deemed arson for hire and insurance fraud. This fire provides a perspective not found in the others because it was solved. Read all the articles written on the fire, and we can discuss it as part of the overall exposé."

"Thank you for your input, and believe it or not, I remember the Foodtown fire because I lived across the street in the Jackson projects. That night the entire Housing Authority community was affected by the loss of Foodtown. Many of us shopped there, and for others, it was the only food store utilized because it was convenient. I was in my junior year in high school when the fire occurred on a Sunday night, filling the projects with smoke. I have an idea where you're going with this issue and will be included in my review."

Newton responded, "Key to solving the case was the insurance investigator who was tenacious, his name was Leo Guzman. The reason I recall some of the facts was I wrote the article covering the fire in 1972. I also want to caution you that I do not have a final decision on whether the article gets published because I will have to present it to the editorial board for final approval. Having said that, I certainly agree with the article process and will do everything I can to get it approved. Please get me the timeline as soon as possible. Finally, just a reminder that you still must complete your regular articles and in a timely manner."

"Thanks, Newton," said Delia as she left his office.

Delia's initial task was to complete the timeline and identify the people who would be interviewed along with potential dates. She listed the interviews in an order that would support the article. The order and potential dates for the interviews were as follows:

Week 1

- Mayor
- Code official
- Fire department representative
- Police department representative

Week 2

- County prosecutor
- FBI representative
- Insurance investigator
- Tenant advocate

Week 3

- A displaced family
- Exposé draft

Delia envisioned devoting two days a week to the interviews with goals of completing four each week. Given that the plan would take approximately one month to complete, the timeline was to begin in mid-December, but it was put off until the first week in January, after the holidays.

On the last week of December, Delia started reaching out to the people on her list to interview beginning in January. Mayor Cappiello's office was the first call she made, requesting an interview date and time. The mayor's secretary returned the call and scheduled Thursday, January 7 at 11:00 a.m. in his office for the interview, with the topic being the fires and gentrification. Delia knew the interview questions had to be prepared and have a defined focus.

The second interview she scheduled was with the code enforcement official Mr. D'onofrio, who she knew was Carol D'onofrio's father, the senior high school student who died in an auto accident returning from the Jersey Shore on Memorial weekend. His secretary informed Delia that he could meet with her on Tuesday January 12 at three thirty, which was the end of his workday. Delia started to realize that if she did not arrange for the interviews to occur sooner, it would take months to complete the exposé. She decided to call all on the list to see who was available for in person interviews or who would opt for phone interviews.

CHAPTER 20

The Interviews

The Mayor

Delia's first interview was with Mayor Cappiello on Thursday January 7 at 11:00 a.m. The mayor's secretary led her into his inner office, where he greeted her warmly, asking her to sit down across from him at a conference table.

"Mayor, thank you for meeting with me this morning. I think we have met on other occasions, but this is my first time in your office."

"Welcome, Ms. Delgado. First, I don't know if my secretary told you, but unfortunately, I must leave for a meeting in the county by eleven thirty to make a twelve-noon meeting."

"I understand, Mayor. Let me start by asking about the fires and arson resulting in deaths and displacements."

The mayor responded, "The fires were an unfortunate reality, which have occurred in Hoboken but have also occurred in other cities throughout the United States. It's more of an inner-city problem. Regarding arson, this is a law enforcement issue, which we take very seriously."

"Both of these issues are perceived in the community, especially among the Hispanic residents, as a nonurgent matter in need of a more proactive measure. How would you respond to that perception?"

"Well, like I said we take it very seriously, but the ultimate responsibility to investigate the arson fires and fatalities fall under the purview of the county prosecutor. As a city, our police and fire department assist them in their investigation. We have also moved forward with requiring smoke detectors in tenement buildings."

"Mayor, people believe you favor condo conversions of tenement buildings."

"First, the condo conversion regulations are from a state law which governs its process. The conversion of older tenement buildings also results in higher revenues for the city. The revenues help to keep the tax rate down, an issue constant in politics. In addition, not all tenement buildings which are or were renovated went to condos, some became subsidized units owned by the Applied Corporation and others."

"Mayor, you have been quoted in other newspapers as placing the blame on the community themselves for the fires saying, 'Family disputes are to blame for the fires and low-income families generate more rubbish than others, causing fires.' You also suggested it could be a cultural issue. Can you elaborate on that?"

"Ms. Delgado, fires are as a result of arson for revenge, kitchen fires, and arson for profits. I think we fall in all those categories, and one reason does not correspond to all."

"Mayor, can you respond to the cultural comment you made, blaming the people themselves for the fire."

"What I said was not meant to offend any of the residents, but rather when people come from different parts of the country, sometimes their customs are different. I also know that poverty limits your options for housing, many of whom live in older tenement buildings."

"Mayor, gentrification has played a major role in the Hoboken fires. Do you agree?"

"No, I believe the fires don't drive gentrification. It's not that simple."

"I'm not saying it's simple, what I am asking, Do you agree there is a correlation between the two."

"Yes, the fires have contributed to gentrification, but economic pressure is a greater rationale for gentrification."

"Mayor, the pressure to vacate apartments is the reason for families being displaced literally by the hundreds the last five years. Landlords have the motivation to deliver tenement buildings vacant resulting in a higher sales price, do you agree?"

"Like I said, economics drive the real estate market. It ebbs and flows."

"Mayor, I know you must go, but I have three more questions, okay? First, you're up for reelection in May. How will you fare?"

"I think the election will prove me right. The city has been moving in the right direction with new housing developments, renovations, and its success has attracted newer residents—all of which is a confirmation of my policies."

"Mayor, do you believe you will get support from low- and moderate-income tenants given the fires and gentrification?"

"Yes, I think the low- and moderate-income families in Hoboken, including the senior citizens, know that the last eight years as mayor and prior to that as councilman, I have supported subsidized housing in Hoboken for over 1,800 apartments found in Applied Housing, Clock Towers, Church Towers, and three new senior citizens buildings. That's the record I'm running on. However, with the election of President Reagan, the cutback on federal subsidies is the greatest challenge facing low- and moderate-incomes families in Hoboken. Without these subsidies, we will see very few affordable units coming online. The fact is, Hoboken has only one hundred Section 8 subsidies left over from the previous president. That's the reality."

"Mayor, many from the Hispanic community believe you are responsible for the fires in Hoboken because of your housing policy favoring condominiums. What is your response to that belief?"

"It's ridiculous. As mayor, I have a responsibility to run this city and maintain the public safety of all our residents. I have done that and lead the city into the future. Presently, I am working with a group of Puerto Rican teachers who are putting together a homeownership and low-income tenant housing development called Caparra Homes. If I were against the community, I would not be supportive of this new project."

"Finally, Mayor, what do you say to the families who lost loved ones in fires the last ten years?"

"Ms. Delgado, thank you for coming in to interview me. The families who lost loved ones have experienced the worst tragedies of their lives. As mayor, I have extended my condolences in the past and will continue to pursue any perpetrator responsible for illegal acts. Thank you again, Ms. Delgado."

Delia left the office with a feeling that the last question did not sit well with the mayor.

On May 5, 1981, Mayor Cappiello was overwhelmingly reelected to a third term virtually unopposed. The outrage against the fires and gentrification did not have a bearing on the election. Delia walked away from the interview with a feeling it was incomplete, and the mayor doubled down on his position that the city had done everything it could in response to the fires.

Building Inspector

Joseph D'onofrio interview was scheduled for Tuesday, January 12, at three thirty in the afternoon. Delia walked directly into his office at city hall as his secretary had left for the day.

"Mr. D'onofrio, good afternoon. Hope you remember me. I'm Delia Delagado from the *Dispatch*, and I knew your daughter from Hoboken High School."

"Yes, I remember. You were very considerate and kind during Carol's funeral."

"Thank you for agreeing to the interview. I am writing an article about the fires and gentrification here in Hoboken. Mr. D'onofrio, my first question is, What role do you play regarding the housing codes of tenement buildings?"

"As building inspection, I'm responsible to monitor that housing units in Hoboken meet all codes approved by the city and state."

"Do you visit these buildings as part of your responsibility?"

"Yes, on a daily basis, I visit up to two buildings a day, and I am a one-man shop."

"Being by yourself, how can you inspect all the buildings in Hoboken, and how do you know which ones to inspect?"

"Let me make a slight correction, the state has a housing division also responsible to inspect especially tenement buildings. They are obligated to complete an inspection of multifamily buildings every five years and issue certificates of inspection approval commonly called green cards. However, they incorporate my inspections in their reports."

"Can you say that all the buildings requiring inspections and corrections are completed in a timely fashion?"

"We try."

"Focusing on older tenements buildings, many of them don't have functional smoke detectors, unlock front doors, and apartment entrance doors do not close automatically, which help to contain a fire. Do you agree that the tenement buildings that experienced deadly fires were in violation of housing codes?"

"The truth is, fires occur in buildings with or without violations."

"That's true. What I am pursuing is how your role can help prevent fatalities in the tenement fires."

"I agree, my role is important but the older tenement buildings in Hoboken cannot be renovated fast enough. The Applied Corporation has helped with renovations and retrofitting them with smoke detectors and sprinkler systems in common areas. These improvements are also found in the newly renovated condominiums as well. The fact is more improvements are needed in the older buildings because inspections are not enough."

"Mr. D'onofrio, my final question is, have you ever been directed to avoid inspecting any buildings?"

"I've never heard of that and would not follow that instruction. The answer is *no*."

"Mr. D'onofrio, thank you for your time."

Delia left the office grateful to have seen and spoken with Mr. D'onofrio. She walked away recognizing he had a difficult job lacking the needed support in manpower to hold more landlords accountable for housing violations.

Fire Department Interview

Delia arranged to meet with deputy fire chief James McLaughlin to discuss the department's effort fighting the Hoboken fires. On Thursday, January 14, she met the deputy chief at his office located at the second and Jefferson Street fire station.

"Deputy Chief, thank you for meeting me this morning. As you are aware, I am writing a comprehensive article for the *Dispatch* on the Hoboken fires, fatalities, and gentrification. The first question is, what is the department's position on all the hundreds of fires which occurred in the last five years?"

"The fire department has responded to all the fires which occur in Hoboken as it is our responsibility. The public counts on us to defend them on mishaps and/or intentional fires."

"From 1973 to the present, Hoboken has experienced fifty-four fire fatalities. Most were children, and the number is above average for a city our size. Does this concern the department?"

"Any fatalities caused by fires are our concern. We are the ones that fight the fires, remove people from burning buildings, and save lives. We also contain fires trying to limit the tenants from losing their homes. The fatalities were unfortunate tragedies caused by various situations. Most fires are caused by the tenants themselves accidentally. You have faulty wiring in the older buildings and, of course, arson. All these reasons contributed to the deaths in our community."

"What measures has the department taken to prevent future deathly fires?"

"First, the city has upgraded the fire department with a new dispatch system, additional firefighters, as well as a new hook-and-ladder truck. Secondly, we have modified our fire training curriculum for all personnel and ranks. Thirdly, we are working with all Hoboken Schools providing training for students on fire prevention safety and responsibilities. We basically have gone beyond drop and roll."

"Do you believe fire-prevention initiatives such as smoke detectors, sprinkler systems, and other fire-code strategies could have prevented the fatalities?"

"Yes, hindsight is 20/20. The fire-prevention items you mention would have had a great impact in saving lives. But the buildings were not appropriately equipped. The fire department has taken a strong position on legally requiring all tenement apartments with smoke detectors. We finally implemented it locally, and it had an impact on state regulations."

"Deputy, a few more questions. If you had the authority to implement changes which would prevent fatalities, what would you do?"

"I shared with you some of the changes we are presently undertaking. However, additional fire prevention personnel, four new fire trucks, require all tenement buildings immediately install smoke detectors, sprinklers systems where necessary, fire extinguishers in all hallways, grease-fire extinguishers in all kitchens, and finally more public awareness of fire preventions. All of these are possible, but at this point, they remain on the drawing board."

"Deputy, do the firefighters have an opinion or perspective on the fires as it affects them?"

"Yes, they certainly like to capture the individuals responsible for the arson fires as it puts them in danger as well. We even found accelerants in some cases before it was used, confirming it was arson. But our initial job was to secure the buildings and saving lives."

"My final question is, our society always recognizes those which go beyond their call of duty and some call them heroes, do you believe firefighters fall into this category?"

"When our firefighters join the department, we accept our role to fight fires and save lives. In addition, courage is one of the traits needed to be a firefighter. Yes, it feels great when we rescue someone from a fire, but we also have a responsibility to attend to the fatalities and their remains, a heart-wrenching moment especially when children are involved. I am a F. Scott Fitzgerald fan and his quote about heroes, "Show me a hero and I will write you a tragedy." I believe it applies to our fires in Hoboken."

The Hoboken Police Department

Delia scheduled the police department interview on Tuesday, January 19. Captain O'Riely was assigned by the chief to meet with her. She went to his office at police headquarters, which was in the lower level of city hall.

"Captain O'Riely, thank you for meeting with me. The article I'm writing is about the Hoboken fires, fatalities, arson, and gentrification. My first question is, most fires involving fatalities were considered arson, was the department involved in trying to solve these cases?"

"Ms. Delgado, the police department has the responsibility to address all criminal activity including arson. We have worked closely with the county prosecutor's office investigating all fires with fatalities related to arson. However, ultimately, the prosecutor's office has the final authority on these investigations."

"It has been reported that some police officers were the first to arrive at fires and had rendered aid to residents. Does the department train all its officers on safety procedures and first aid?"

"Yes, we are often the first to arrive and provide assistance. We have anecdotes of officers knocking on doors to alert and remove tenants from burning buildings. Secondly, all our officers are trained in first aid and carry oxygen tanks in all vehicles."

"Captain, has the department taken any proactive steps to apprehend arson suspects and/or monitor tenement buildings which have been threatened with arson?"

"The department patrols the entire city and cannot assign personnel to all tenement buildings. Nevertheless, the fact that we patrol with mark and unmarked vehicles has deterred criminal action such as arson. Any building site that has been threatened with arson is investigated and closely watched by our patrols."

"Arson has affected the Puerto Rican community on a disproportional basis. Many in the community expressed concern that the city is not doing enough to address the fires and arrest. Can you comment on that?"

"As I indicated, we are patrolling all parts of the city including the tenement buildings where many Hispanic families live. We do not distinguish between ethnic backgrounds regarding any crime or arson."

"Captain, to follow up on the last question, has the department taken any steps to bridge the gap of confidence between the department and the Hispanic community?"

"Yes, the department ten years ago did not have the diversity we have today. We now have twelve officers of minority backgrounds and are pending new recruits, which include officers of Hispanic background. In addition, the department has adopted a community outreach curriculum with the schools focusing on public safety and careers."

"Final question, do you believe that an organized gentrification effort exists to burn residents out of their tenement apartments?"

"We have not come to that conclusion and have not seen that type of criminal pattern. However, the open cases of arson are ongoing."

"Just let me ask a follow-up question. Does that mean the suspected unsolved arson cases which had fatalities are deemed open homicide cases?"

"The prosecutor is the one that determines a homicide case, and as you know, homicide cases have no statute of limitations."

"Finally, let me thank you for helping me and my family when we experienced the threat."

Delia left the police headquarters returning to the *Dispatch* and gave Newton an update on the interview completed so far. Her next interview would be a phone call with the county prosecutor's public affairs representative the following week.

The Hudson County Prosecutor's Office

The next interview Delia scheduled was with the Hudson County prosecutor's public information officer. It was a phone call interview scheduled for Thursday, January 21, at 11:00 a.m. The public information officer was Ms. Linda Howard, who represented the prosecutor Harold Ruvoldt Jr.

"Ms. Howard, thank you for this opportunity. As you are aware, I am writing a comprehensive article for the

Hudson Dispatch on the fires, fatalities, and gentrification. My first question is, What role does the prosecutor's office play regarding fatal fires in Hoboken?"

"The office of Hudson County prosecutor has a countywide responsibility to assist in homicides and other felonies committed within our boundaries. We work with local municipal police and commit to assure prosecutions are completed as per the law. Regarding the Hoboken fires, we have had prosecutor investigators examine arson claims and other cases such as insurance fraud."

"You mentioned homicides. Does the prosecutor identify arson related fire fatalities cases that are not solved as open cases?"

"First, arson cases need to be certified as deliberate fires by either the Hoboken Fire Department and/or our investigators. Once it is established as arson, any fatalities would be considered homicide. The second part is, once a homicide investigation is established, if not solved technically, it remains open."

"The county prosecutor was quoted in another newspaper as describing the fires as 'difficult to solve and most are not arson related but rather caused by the tenants themselves.' This statement suggested the fatalities were tenants' fault even though the fire department indicated arson."

"The county prosecutor takes his role very seriously, and the investigations look at all cases they are required to do. When he says the cases are difficult to solve, it's because, statistically, not only in Hudson County but throughout urban centers, arson fires have low conviction rates."

"The prosecutor seems to extend the blame of fires to tenants and their cultures. Is that the official position?"

"I cannot confirm the quote you mention, but Hudson County is made up of different cultures, yet we investigate all complaints that fall within our purview regardless of culture, creed and race."

"My final question is cultural related. The Puerto Rican community in Hoboken believe they are targets of these fires, have the greatest number of fatalities, and represent the group most affected by gentrification. A lack of confidence exists in enforcing code regulations and arson prevention measures. Does the prosecutor have a role in addressing these concerns?"

"The prosecutor is the highest law enforcement officer in the county. As such, he supersedes local authorities on criminal prosecution. However, he recognizes that local authorities cooperate with our office in most cases, and we rely on their input to secure convictions. We cannot, however, be expected to dismiss their authority, only the state attorney general has that power."

"Do you have any comments for the Hispanic community in Hoboken?"

"We will and have responded to any official complaint that reaches this office. Mr. Rouvolt is aware of their concerns and will continue to operate his office effectively for all residents of Hudson County."

"Thank you, Ms. Howard you have been very helpful. Please thank Prosecutor Rouvolt for allowing this interview. Thank you again, goodbye."

Delia ended her phone conversation with Ms. Howard feeling she had answered all the questions. Although it was her first phone interview, she felt it was successful and provided valuable insight. This represented her fifth interview completed, and she began to prepare for her next one with the Justice Department, including their investigative arm, the FBI.

The Justice Department and FBI

Delia's effort to interview the Justice Department representative was based on her belief that the federal government had a role to play in investigating unsolved arson cases and fatalities. The question she was seeking an answer to was whether federal laws were violated under the Civil Rights Act. She contacted their Newark office looking to arrange an in-person meeting. She reached their spokesperson and scheduled to meet with them on Tuesday, January 26, at 10:30 a.m. located in the Federal Plaza building in Newark, New Jersey.

She also arranged to meet the insurance investigator who handled the 1972 Foodtown fire and the more recent Markum fire. Mr. Leo Guzman was key in solving these cases and others in northern New Jersey. The interview would be at 2:00 p.m. the same day as the Justice Department since his office was also located in Newark at the new Gateway complex adjacent to Penn Station.

On the day of the interviews, Delia took the PATH train from Hoboken to Newark Penn Station. She walked to the Federal building, which was five blocks from the train station.

Arriving at the building, she entered and went directly to the public information office and asked to see Mr. John Raymond, who was the acting public relation officer.

"Good morning, Ms. Delgado, welcome to our office. Did you have any problem finding us?"

"No, I walked directly from the train station, only a few blocks away."

"Very good. What can I do for you?"

"Mr. Raymond, as you know, I am a reporter for the *Hudson Dispatch*, and I am writing an extensive article on the fires, fatalities, and gentrification. My first question is whether the Department of Justice have any jurisdiction in Hoboken regarding the arson fires which resulted in deaths?"

"The Department of Justice as a federal entity has the authority to enter any jurisdiction they identify affecting federal law."

"Yes, I understand that, but did the department and/or the FBI look into the situation of fires and fifty plus fatalities experienced in Hoboken the last ten years?"

"These unfortunate fires are within the responsibility of local law enforcement including the county prosecutor, not our department."

"The Hispanic community have suffered the majority of fatalities and thousands of families have been displaced. Does this fall under any civil rights protections?"

"The Justice Department would investigate any concerns raised which has an appearance of violating federal statues including civil rights."

"Does this mean no one has reached out to the department, therefore it has not been investigated?"

"Ms. Delgado, it sounds as if you are raising the issue and not the community."

"No, I am just acquiring information that would be helpful to understand why the department has or has not looked into the Hoboken arson fires."

"The department has many investigations going on at the same time, and I cannot confirm that this issue is one of them."

"As the investigatory arm of the DOJ, the FBI had been involved in solving an arson case in Hoboken in the past, which included an organized crime figure."

"Ms. Delgado, the FBI does serve as our investigatory division and have been involved on cases daily. I am not surprised they helped to solve the case because it involved organized crime. However, they had to be invited to get involved."

"It was my understanding that the insurance company requested the agency get involved in that case. My next question is whether the department will examine the situation in Hoboken? If yes, would this case be referred to the civil rights division?"

"We are amenable to look at the Hoboken fires, and after the review, we would determine its merits as well as what division should handle it."

"Mr. Raymond, my final question or statement is, the low-income minority community of Hoboken occupy most of the tenement buildings. They live in fear of arson fires, thinking they could be next. Many have children, and the majority of those killed in the fires have been children. What can the department say or do to allay their fear?"

"The Justice Department will investigate any entity that violates federal laws including governmental agencies. We will do our best to examine this situation."

Delia thanked Mr. Raymond for his cooperation and shared her confidence in the Justice Department. Her interview ended around eleven thirty, leaving plenty of time for lunch and returning to the Gateway building at Penn Station. She reviewed her notes over lunch and believed the DOJ had not looked at the Hoboken situation as something they should get involved with it. However, she hoped they would investigate the Hoboken fires, which up to this point, they unfortunately chose not to get involved.

Leo Guzman

Delia made her way back from the Federal building to the Gateway office complex around one thirty, and she headed directly to Leo Guzman's office located on the fifth floor. Approaching his front door, Delia saw the sign, which read, "Private Investigator-Consultant." For her, it was something out of a movie to meet a real private eye. She expected Philip Marrow upon entering but did not see Mr. Guzman directly as he was in the inner office, absent his secretary.

"Mr. Guzman, it's Ms. Delgado. Can I come in?"

He responded, "Please. I am at my desk."

She entered and met Mr. Guzman, a slightly overweight middle-aged individual, not a Hollywood figure.

"Hi, Mr. Guzman. I'm Delia Delgado from the *Hudson Dispatch*," Delia said as she shook his hand. "Very nice meeting you."

"Welcome, did you have a problem getting here," said Guzman.

"No, as I told you this morning, I met with the representative of the Justice Department and walked back to your office."

"Very good. My secretary left for the day. She only works part time. Are you Hispanic, Ms. Delgado?"

"Yes, I'm Puerto Rican."

"My parents came from Puerto Rico also," said Guzman. "Making me Boricua like you. Let's get started."

"First, let me say I never met a real-life PI. Having said that, I work for the *Hudson Dispatch*." She showed him her credential. "I am writing a comprehensive article about the Hoboken fires, fatalities, and gentrification."

"Oh, it is a sad situation in Hoboken, especially for the Puerto Rican community and others who live in apartment buildings."

"I know. That's why I am writing this article hoping to cover as many elements as possible which have affected the community fires. The first question I have—"

Mr. Guzman interrupted her and said, "Can I first ask why you want to interview me?"

"Good question. In my research, I found that ten years ago, you were working for the Prudential Insurance company as an investigator and you were instrumental in solving an arson for hire case in Hoboken. It's my understanding that the Foodtown fire on Third and Jackson Street would not have been solved without you. In addition, you were or are involved with the Markum fire investigation."

"Thanks for that, I remember the Foodtown case well. It was, in fact, arson for hire and involved an organized crime figure. However, the Markum case is more recent and still has some pending issues, so I cannot comment."

"Okay, let me first ask you about your professional experiences and how you came to become such an expert on fires and how you ended up working for Prudential?"

"When I came back from the war, WWII, I was interested in law enforcement and was able to join the Newark Police Department. After fifteen years as a regular police officer, I was promoted to detective assigned to a special fraud division. In 1967, Newark had riots, and I was asked to train in arson fire investigation as it related to fraud."

"So you consider yourself an expert in arson fires and fraud?"

"Yes. In 1970, I retired from the police department and accepted a job with Prudential Insurance to work on insurance fraud related to fires. The fact is, not all landlords get away with insurance fraud when we investigate."

"That brings me back to the Foodtown fire. What happened in that case?"

"I remember receiving a call from my supervisor assigning me to the Foodtown case in Hoboken. Two days after the fire, I went to examine the building, and the firefighters allowed me to walk around the interior showing me where they thought the fire started. They believed it had started as a result of a break-in burglary igniting the fire by the safe. In further examination, I found signs of an accelerant on the other side of the building. When I inquired with the firefighters, they said, 'That's why we called you.'"

"Did you conclude it was arson?"

"I collected as much evidence possible but knew only law enforcement entities could solve this case. I had seen other cases like this one where the arsonist tries to cover up their steps by creating an alternate rational for the fire. I am good friends with an FBI agent who joined the investigation based on my recommendation that it appeared to be arson for profit, an organized crime method."

"Can you give me the name of the FBI agent?"

"He retired from the agency three years ago and moved to Florida. So the answer to that question is no. However, between the agent, the Hoboken police, and myself, we were able to narrow it down to a few suspects. Ultimately, good detective work resulted in the arrest of the right suspect."

"Was he from Hoboken?"

"No, it turned out he lived in Newark and was considered an associate of the Gambino crime family. It was an arson-for-hire case and insurance fraud."

"Who hired him?"

"He wouldn't say, although I believe it was an inside job. The perpetrator was convicted and sentenced to prison, and it led to the recovery of insurance money."

"Job well done! That's what this interview is all about, your skills and the FBI involvement were instrumental in solving the case. The present situation in Hoboken is rampant and in need of closure. Are you presently working in Hoboken regarding any of the fires besides the Markum?"

"I hesitate to answer that because I am an independent consultant for different insurance companies and cannot divulge that information. For me to talk about a pending case could compromise it and result in me losing business."

"I understand, but what if it was off the record and I cannot directly use it in my article?"

"How can I be sure, I just met you?"

"Okay, but before I leave that issue, you know that over fifty people died in fires of which most were children and of Puerto Rican background."

"Look, it's very emotional, I know. Let me say this, most building owners have mortgages and insurance including in Hoboken. That's all I can say."

"I understand. My last question is, Have you ever solved an arson case in an apartment building resulting in insurance fraud?"

"Yes, I believe those cases may be difficult to solve, but not impossible. I learned when I was working as a Newark detective and presently as an insurance investigator that perpetrators make mistakes, leaving clues. If the insurance company feels a case cannot be solved, they do not expend the effort to investigate. Ms. Delgado, I must end this conversation at this time. Thank you for stopping by. Please send me a copy of your article when completed and published."

"Thank you, Mr. Guzman."

Delia left and caught the next PATH train back to Hoboken.

Immediately after arriving from Newark, Delia began to line up what she thought was her last interviews. First, she would arrange to meet with a tenant advocate and community organizer, Mr. Johnny Garcia. Secondly, she envisioned identifying a displaced fire victim to get their perspective on the fires and gentrification. She contacted Garcia and scheduled to meet him in his office on Friday, the twenty-ninth, at 11:00 a.m. She also requested him to have a displaced tenant that same day so she could interview as well. He agreed.

On the same afternoon, while in her office preparing for the last two interviews, she received a call from Mr. Guzman.

"Ms. Delgado?"

"Yes."

"This is Mr. Guzman. How are you, and are you available to meet me tomorrow in Hoboken?"

"Tomorrow?"

"Yes, I'll be in Hoboken, and I think we should meet. I have more information you can use."

"Okay, what time and where?"

"How about the coffee shop on Newark and Bloomfield Street, behind city hall, say at ten thirty?"

"Good, I'll see you then."

Delia did not know what to think about the call other than perhaps she got to him with the last question.

The following day Delia met Guzman at the coffee shop, and they greeted each other warmly.

"Mr. Guzman, thank you for calling me. I thought you could not say anything else?"

"You're right. But as an investigator, I did some homework and looked up the articles you had written about the fires, and I got to thinking I could trust you."

"Thank you. As you said, I am committed to writing this article or exposé with as much verifiable information as possible."

"All right, I called you because I agree the community needs help. And it's true, I am working here in Hoboken on a few cases. However, I must ask you to keep my name out of any article relevant to my investigations. The particulars I am sure you will find very interesting, and it has to do with arson for hire. We have been investigating three insurance claims of apartments building totaling approximately $500,000.00. Then the landlord has arranged to sell the property collecting another $500,000. Some would say it's a good business model, but when it involves arson for hire its fraud. Have you ever heard of Michael Gusto or Vinny Bernardo?"

"Oh no, you have got to be kidding me. The answer is yes."

"Mr. Gusto owned the three buildings we insured, and we are looking at him and his nephew Vinny who manages the property. It turns out—again, I'm telling you this off the record—that Vinny was being watched by the FBI because of his uncle's business dealings and his drug transactions. The FBI part is confidential and off the record."

"How can I verify that this is true, especially the FBI investigation? In addition, you know Vinny was killed."

"I know he was killed, and the case is still pending. However, I am not sure how you can verify what I told you. The only way I think it can is if my friend from the FBI talks to you. I would need to call him in Florida first to see if he would be amenable to speak to you off the record. I will call you next week about that."

"Okay, good."

"Anyway, they were following Vinny one night as part of their organized crime investigation, and he led them to one of the buildings Gusto owns. He entered, and within fifteen minutes, he came running out rather quickly. The FBI agent said smoke began to fill the building shortly thereafter and the residents were running out. The agents followed Vinny for three blocks and then picked him up, informing him they saw him coming out of the burning building. They took him back to their Newark office and threatened to arrest him for arson and possible murder if he did not cooperate with them. The agents were interested in his uncle's organized crime activity and would forget about the fires in exchange for his cooperation."

"Wait, so they saw him come out of a building that was burning?"

"You got it."

"But why did it not surface that he was caught?"

"That's the point. They did not arrest him, you see, because that was not their goal. The case they were building was loan sharking, illegal gambling, and drugs, not arson."

"Are you telling me they placed their case ahead of the fatal fires?"

"Basically, they had him on arson but rather told him to cooperate with them or he could get life in prison for the fires. It was enough for Vinny to flip and become an informant for the FBI."

"That is some story. I don't know for sure if I can use it in my article."

"Certainly not, exactly like I told you. But if you can confirm that the FBI is investigating the fires, it would help your article."

"You're right, but you know Vinny was killed last year, and although they said it was foul play, no one has been arrested."

"I know the agency believes it was a mob hit, but they were putting out there it was drug related. Unfortunately, with his death, the case for arson is just about lost, and the organized crime case is also hampered. Let me leave you with this though. What I told you today is accurate, and if I can arrange for you to speak with the retired agent, you will need to speak with your law department to see if it can be used perhaps as a confidential source. Again, I will call you next week after I speak with him. One more thing, my friend did not agree with letting Vinny slide on the arson in exchange for him to become an informant. That decision was made by his superiors over his objection. He retired a few years later after only twenty years as an agent, early retirement. Finally, did you know that Deep Throat, the informant used by the *Washington Post* for the Watergate investigation was, in fact, an FBI agent? It will come out someday."

"Great, I will check with my editor and give the law department a heads up on what we spoke about. Mr. Guzman, I cannot thank you enough. You have been a valuable source, and this has been a learning experience. God bless you."

"Bendicion."

They left the coffee shop together and parted ways.

The information provided by Guzman was an incredible revelation for Delia. Up to that point, she knew landlords were taking advantage of the fires to vacate their properties and would double their profit by selling the property. To Delia, it appeared as a sinister approach to a business model. The problem she had was, how this and Guzman's information could be verified for the article. It required her to meet with Newton and explain how she obtained the information.

The next day she met with Newton to share the information related to Mr. Guzman's story. Newton listened attentively about the FBI investigation and how they stumbled into the arson case. It was difficult for Newton to fathom that a choice was made to pursue the organized crime angle over the arson. Delia suggested that she can claim to have received the information from a reliable confidential source and include it in the article. Newton, however, did not agree, saying that without the direct confirmation from the retired FBI agent, it would be speculation, unacceptable. Newton did ask her to start writing the article and he would review it. He also expected that the *Dispatch* law department and the editorial board would need to approve it for print.

Delia returned to her desk knowing it was a challenging process for her to utilize all the information collected. She believed it would be necessary to include Guzman's revelations for it to be an effective article. The fact was she still had two more interviews to complete before she would write the draft, including John Garcia and a displaced family, both scheduled for the following day.

John Garcia Interview

John Garcia was a tenant advocate heading his own not-for-profit organization in Hoboken. He had grown up in New York City of Puerto Rican background but had resided in Hoboken for the past fifteen years. Recently, he had organized a demonstration to city hall protesting the fires and gentrification affecting low-income tenants.

Delia arrived at his store front office at 11:00 a.m. as planned and went directly into the interview.

"Mr. Garcia, very nice meeting you. I saw you at the demonstration, and it was a successful statement about the community problems."

"It was a necessary action. Some think it was long in coming. However, I am afraid it needs to be continued. The fires and many of the families who suffered the losses have reached out to me expressing their sadness and anger. They seek justice for what has happened to them and the Hispanic community in general. I'm not an attorney, but I believe the city abdicated their responsibility on this issue."

"Mr. Garcia, what do you see as a solution to the problems?"

"I don't know what could correct the tragedies that have occurred in Hoboken. I do know some people or someone has to answer for it."

"Your organization is tenant oriented, raising the issue of gentrification toward low-income families. It appears that the trend to remove tenants from their homes cannot be stopped. Is there a solution that you can think would counter this trend?"

"I advocate for people to stay in their homes and let the landlords force them out, or for that matter pay them to leave."

"You describe the landlord effort to provide incentives for tenants to leave as an inadequate exchange for a home."

"Yes, its petty cash for the landlords or developers, an insult to our community."

"Mr. Garcia, what do you see is the future for the Puerto Rican community in Hoboken and low-income tenants in general?"

"It's obvious the choices are limited. Stay and fight taking the landlords to court, take their money and move, get a subsidized apartment at Applied or the Housing Authority. Unfortunately, both of those entities have vacancy rates of 1 percent, and there are no signs it will change. Let me also make a prediction—the pressures will happen someday to eliminate or reduce the projects and subsidies at Applied Housing will end."

"That last part is a bold and a sad prediction."

"It's what I believe. Where is the outrage by the general population? There isn't any. Recently, the community overwhelmingly reelected the mayor, sending a message that the city was heading in the right direction despite the gentrification, and there was no political outrage for the fifty plus people who died."

"Mr. Garcia, how long will your organization last and will the fight for tenants continue?"

"That's a good question. I predict the problem of gentrification will not stop at the low-income tenant's door. But rather, it will affect the moderate-income tenants such as city workers, police, firefighters, and teachers who will have a difficult time finding affordable housing. The only factor absent for them will be the fires fueling the gentrification. The other reality is that the political will to ensure that all tenement buildings have fire measures like smoke detectors is absent and would have prevented fatalities, a real tragedy."

"Mr. Garcia, thank you for your insight. The predictions are quite interesting. Does that mean good planning on the city part can avoid the shortages of affordable moderate-income housing in the future?"

"No. It's inevitable, I believe. Okay, I set up a meeting with you and Mrs. Torres. She was a tenant of the Clinton Street fires and survived because she and her two kids lived on the first floor. If you follow me, Ms. Delgado, she is waiting for you in the next office."

Mrs. Torres Interview

Mr. Garcia introduced Delia to Mrs. Santa Torres and left the office so they could talk.

"Mrs. Torres, very nice meeting you. My name is Delia Delgado, and I am a reporter for the *Hudson Dispatch*. I am writing an article about the Hoboken fires, fatalities, and gentrification. You are in a very unique position to talk about all three areas and the fact that you are of Hispanic background, correct?"

"Yes, I was born in Santurce, Puerto Rico, but grew up here in New Jersey. However, what happened to us in Hoboken was the worst thing that we experienced in our lives. I have two young kids, and it breaks my heart just thinking about what they went through. You're right, I can speak about all three items you mentioned, but ask me one at a time."

"Okay, tell me about the experience you and your children went through when your building caught fire."

"It was the worst day in our lives, and we will never forget it. We were living at 129 Clinton Street, a railroad flat with very little heat, so we slept together in the same bedroom, warmest room in the apartment. That night of January 29, 1979, about one thirty in the morning, we were awakened to screams, 'Fuego, fire!' At first, I didn't know what to do other than grab my kids. We were lucky living on the first floor of the tenement building. The smoke started to fill the apartment, but we managed to grab our coats and run out the front door. We could hear the other tenants screaming and also running out. It was horrible. My kids were coughing and crying at the same time. They didn't know exactly what was happening as they were half asleep. Ms. Delgado, I am sorry, but I need some water, or I will just break down and cry."

Delia returned to the room with a bottle of water provided by Mr. Garcia and asked if she was willing to continue the interview.

"Yes, I was talking about my children. I had the responsibility to explain what was happening without depressing them more than they were. The flames were shooting out of the top two floors and had engulfed the entire building within the first five minutes. I struggled to tell my kids what we faced next, knowing we had nothing left and had lost our home. However, I felt so blessed that we were all safe."

"Let me interject and ask you to speak about what you call home."

"Yes, the apartment was our home. Some people define their homes as where they live and own, for us the apartment was where the kids and I lived, slept, returned from school, watched TV, and shared their day. We lost our home."

"Did you know your neighbors?"

"Yes, I felt absolutely devastated about the family on the top floor at 131 Clinton Street, the building next door to ours. All seventeen died in the fire. That night the Red Cross placed us at the Holiday Inn by the Holland Tunnel. I was glad we were located close to Hoboken and the children could walk to school."

"You lost your home and had to move. Did you ever think your building would be repaired and your family would return?"

"That was wishful thinking on our part. The building next door could not be saved, but our building was boarded up with the landlord looking to sell it as is."

"You basically were displaced and added to the roles of gentrification by fire."

"Yes, at first, I did not know what the word meant, 'gentrification.' Today when I share my story, I use the term gentrification by fire when describing our experience."

"Mrs. Torres, can you speak about your kids? Have they ever talked to you about that night and their whole experience?"

"Thinking about my two kids and what they went through breaks my heart still to this day every time I speak about it. They both were more concerned for me getting through the saga than themselves. Jose, my oldest, was nine at the time and tells me he passes by the neighborhood and thinks about the fire. However, he also told me the buildings were being renovated into condos. He said, 'Ma, I would never buy one of those condos, even if they gave it to me because of the bad memories.' My younger daughter, who was five years old at the time, really does not remember it all. And I think it's good."

"Mrs. Torres, where did you move to after the fire, and where do you live now?"

"From the Holiday Inn, we were able to stay at a cousin's house on Willow Avenue in Hoboken. She was a lifesaver. Family can do what others sometimes can't. At that point, we were basically staying in her living room until we could secure another apartment. One day, shortly after the fire, a neighbor told me to see a housing authority commissioner he knew who could help me get an apartment in the projects. I went to see him at the school he was working at and explained my situation. Within a month, he arranged an apartment for us in the projects. The only problem was, the apartment available was a one-bedroom. Nevertheless, it was better than nothing. The first night my kids and I spent at our new apartment on Marshal Drive was comforting. We felt safe and had an opportunity to start all over again in a new home. The fear we had living in the tenement building at Clinton Street was gone. I still think of the families throughout Hoboken who lost their relatives, especially the children. The fact is, I could not have survived the experience without my children."

"Mrs. Torres, you have been by far the most important person I interviewed," said Delia as tears ran down her face. "Thank you so much."

After completing the interview with Mrs. Torres, Delia though it would be a great opportunity to interview her son, who was at the outer office waiting for his mother.

"Mrs. Torres, is it okay if I ask your son about what he remembers?"

"Yes, sure. He's a bright kid."

Jose Torres Interview

"Jose, thank you for meeting with me. I'm Delia Delgado and I work for the *Hudson Dispatch* newspaper, but you can call me Delia."

"Okay."

"First, how old are you Jose?"

"I'm eleven, going on twelve years old."

"Very good, your mother said it was all right to speak to you."

"Yes."

"Okay, I want to talk about the fires at 129–131 Clinton Street two years ago and ask if you can share what you remember when you were nine years old?"

"Yes."

"What do you remember about that night?"

"I was sleeping in the bedroom with my mother and little sister when I heard people yelling, 'Fuego.' I didn't know what was happening. But my mother started getting us, dressed fast, grabbed our coats, telling us to stay together."

"Did she lead you out the door or window?"

"No, we went out the front door although there was smoke everywhere. I was half asleep when it happened, and the worst thing I saw was when we got outside."

"What did you see that affected you?"

"When we got out the door, I saw our neighbor lady from the upper floor lying on the sidewalk. She had jumped from the second-floor window. I also looked up to the other floors and saw her husband hanging halfway out the window screaming for help."

"Then what happened?"

"My mother took us across the street. Good thing she had grabbed our coats, it was very cold that night. When we crossed the street, we looked back. The building was filled with smoke and fire. By that time, the firemen had arrived and started to pour water on the building. I thought all of our neighbors had escaped the fire, but I found out from my mother, some did not make it."

"How was your mother during all this?"

"My mother looked very sad and glad at the same time because she saved us, but I knew my mother was worried about everything else."

"What do you mean everything else?"

"Where we would live, did we lose all our furniture and clothes?"

"Did you say anything to your mother?"

"Yes, I told her not to worry, we'll be okay. I had prayed, and it's going to be all right. I also told her my sister and I loved her."

"Where did you go next?"

"A person from the Red Cross took us to the Holiday Inn in Jersey City and gave us a room."

"Jose, you are a brave and intelligent kid. This is your last question. What do you think happened that night?"

"A bad man or two burned our building and home. They had no good reason to do that. I loved where we were living and the school I attended, along with my teachers. I will never forget what happened to us and will always thank my mother for saving our lives."

"Jose, thank you for your help."

Delia thanked Mrs. Torres; her son, Jose; and Mr. Garcia for their interviews and promised to share the article when it came out. She returned to her office and reviewed the notes taken during the interviews.

In reflecting on Mrs. Torres's interview, where she expressed her concern at night for her children's safety, Delia was reminded of her art history that included Norman Rockwell paintings and contemporary prints. The one which came to mine was "The freedom of fear." It had appeared in *The Saturday Evening Post* of 1943 and had been inspired by President Roosevelt in a speech to Congress in 1941 on the four American Freedoms. She correlated the drawings to the fears of the Hoboken fires. What was most relevant to her feelings was the print that showed parents hovering over their children they had put to bed and worrying for their safety. The relevancy was startling.

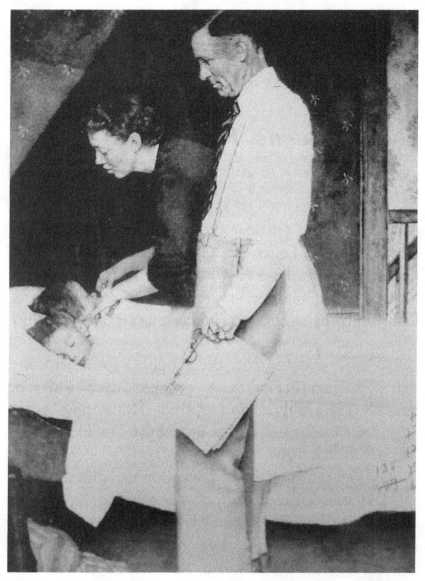

Norman Rockwell, *Freedom of Fear*. Courtesy
of *the Saturday Evening Post*, 1943

CHAPTER 21

Lester Beene, Retired FBI Agent

A week after Leo Guzman's interview, he called Delia to provide her with Lester Beene's telephone number. Beene, Leo's friend, was the retired FBI agent that had provided him with the information regarding Vinny Bernardo. Lester and other agents were building a case mainly against Vinny's uncle, Gasto.

"Delia," said Leo over the phone, "I spoke with my retired FBI friend in Florida, and he agreed to speak with you, but only if he could remain anonymous. Is that possible?"

"Yes, I can quote him as an anonymous source with FBI ties. Is that okay?"

"When you speak to him, mention that phrase."

Leo provided Delia with Beene's telephone number in Winter Gardens, Florida, and Delia indicated she would call him on the weekend.

On Saturday, Delia called Beene at his Florida home where he lived with his wife.

"Mr. Beene, this is Ms. Delia Delgado from the *Hudson Dispatch* in Hoboken, New Jersey. I had spoken with Leo Guzman regarding reaching out to you, and he gave me your telephone number. I hope this is a good time to speak."

"Yes, Ms. Delgado, Leo let me know you would be calling me. He said you wanted to speak about Hoboken, correct?"

"Yes, but specifically about the Hoboken fires of 1970s. I am writing an extensive article about these fires and I believe, based on my conversation with Leo, you may have valuable information to contribute."

"Ms. Delgado, I am a retired FBI agent and probably should not comment officially on any investigation I was involved in."

Delia recognized that her training and experience as an effective reporter would need to be utilized at this time to convince Beene to cooperate.

"Mr. Beene, I am aware that as a former agent, your commitment to the agency is important. However, as indicated by Leo, you have firsthand knowledge of a situation regarding the fires of Hoboken. Let me say this, I am willing to quote an anonymous source if in fact I use any part of this conversation. In fact, if you choose not to proceed, I will honor your request."

"Ms. Delgado, you understand why I hesitate to get involved. I still have friends and colleagues in the business."

"Let me say this, Mr. Beene, I guarantee you are not the first nor will you be the last FBI agent that speaks or provides information to the media regarding a case."

"Ms. Delgado, you are right and persistent. If Leo believes you can be trusted to keep my name out of it, then I will speak with you."

"Thank you, Mr. Beene. The information provided to me indicated you observed Vinny Bernardo leaving a burning building in Hoboken and that you saw this as part of your investigation of organized crime. Is that correct?"

"I hesitate to say it, but that's correct. My partner and I were following Vinny as part of the investigation one night and saw him running from a burning building that he managed."

"So you can confirm that he had been involved with arson?"

"Technically, we could not say for sure, but it did look like it. We followed him for a few blocks before we apprehended him. We took him back to our headquarters in Newark, as per our supervisor's instructions."

"Why wasn't he immediately arrested and taken to the local police headquarters?"

"As I said, my supervisor instructed us to bring him to our headquarters."

"Why would he do that?"

"The supervisor wanted us to use what we observed as leverage against Vinny, to get him to cooperate. He had us offer Vinny an ultimatum, either to cooperate with us and become an informant or he could face arson charges, which could lead to murder if anyone was killed in the fire. The goal was to get Vinny to inform on his uncle and other associates regarding the gambling, loan sharking, and drug activities. The choice was given to Vinny, and he became an informant that evening, willing to wear a wire if need be."

"That is an incredible story, although I believe every bit of it. Did you agree with the instructions when your supervisor told you to forget about Vinny running from the burning building?"

"Not at first, I objected because it was not right for us to ignore the arson that took place even if no one got hurt."

"But you eventually went along with it, correct?"

"My supervisor gave us a direct order, and it was expected to be followed. It was not my finest moment."

"Mr. Beene, I know it was very difficult to tell that story, but it does confirm what you told Leo. The fact is, I may not be able to include it directly in my article. However, it would support my claim that the FBI could have played an important role in solving perhaps some of the arson fires in Hoboken. The truth is, the people of our community were counting on all law enforcement entities to help in solving the arson cases, and the FBI basically let us down. Your confirmation provided the support needed for the newspaper to make some bold statements about the fires. However, again I reiterate my commitment to not use your name other than an anonymous but reliable source. I believe the FBI could have made a difference in solving some of the arson cases, not only those with fatalities, but also fires that caused the exit of thousands of residents from Hoboken via gentrification by fire. Something as simple as letting it be known that the agency was investigating the fires in Hoboken, it would have acted as an effective deterrent possibly saving lives."

Delia thanked Mr. Beene for his cooperation and assured him she would send him a copy of the article.

CHAPTER 22

Jesus Wept

Father Joseph Interview

Delia believed the interviews were complete and would provide an in-depth perspective for the exposé. However, after attending church on Sunday and hearing Father Joseph speak about our responsibility to our brothers, she decided to add him to the interview list. She knew, going back to 1973, that he led a group of parishioners and others, including her parents, in prayers at the Eleventh Street fire. He was present at just about all the fatal fires, meeting with families and providing counseling. She called the following day and made arrangement to meet with him at the rectory for his interview.

"Father Joseph, thank you for meeting with me and allowing me to interview you about the Hoboken fires. First, this interview will not appear in the newspaper directly but will serve as background and resource to an article I am writing regarding the Hoboken fires of 1973 to the present. Okay?"

"Yes, that's fine with me, Delia. I trust you will keep your word."

"Thank you, Father. I would like to start with a question about counseling families from your parish who were affected by the fires and gentrification. What did you say to those families that lost their homes and, in some cases, love ones?"

"I have counseled families for the past ten years regarding the fires which destroyed their homes and requiring them to move out of Hoboken. It was difficult counseling them and providing spiritual guidance when they seem to have lost everything. For the children, they lost their homes, school, teachers, friends, and church. However, through prayer and sharing the hope that exist through God, they will survive this challenge in life. But the most difficult cases I counseled were those families who lost love ones in the fires, many of them have also lost faith and hope. For them, loved ones have been lost, and life as they know it will never return. Sometimes I am moved along with the families and share in their grief. My responsibility at that time is to share God's grace with them and give them reasons to continue, not an easy task."

"Father Joseph, how many families have you had to counsel about the fires?"

"Since the 1973 fatal fire, there have been hundreds of fires in Hoboken, and it seemed like once a week I was talking to a family."

"Father, what impact has gentrification in Hoboken had on St. Joseph Church?"

"Good question, as families lose their homes, most relocate to other communities and seek out parishes closer to their new home. So yes, we have lost about one-third of our parish to gentrification. The fires especially have had major impact on our Spanish-speaking parishioners. And that, combined with the loss of faith by many young people, the church's overall population is on a decline. You know we are closing St. Joseph school in a year because we cannot afford it and the drop in enrollment also related to the fires. Basically, the gentrification by fire hit the children population the most."

"Father Joseph, what is your personal feeling about the fires?"

"Well, I try not to impose my personal feelings with my responsibility as a priest. I set that aside because God ask us to use the wisdom he blessed us with for the good. So I try to find the blessing in the rubble and the salvation in our heart."

"Final question, Father, is, What do you say to the community of Hoboken about the fires?"

"I pray every day for the church, the community and its leaders, asking God for strength and guidance. But I am angered by the fires especially those with fatalities of children. I ended up calling the bishop and asked him to pray for our community. He did. Let me end by quoting the scriptures John 11:35, "Jesus wept." He wept out of empathy for Mary and Martha losing their brother and Jesus losing his friend Lazarus. If He wept, so should we."

CHAPTER 23

The Homeless Shelter and St. Mary's Hospital

The Shelter

In January 1982, Delia wrote several articles about the shelter's startup in Hoboken by the Clergy Coalition and St. Mary's Hospital. In the first article about the shelter, she believed the topic needed to be covered because a segment of residents, mainly single individuals, were not being considered in the discussion of gentrification. The Clergy Coalition, comprised of clergy members for various Hoboken religions, made it their mission to address the issue head on by creating a homeless shelter. The fact was Hoboken's gentrification had an impact on families, seniors, and single individuals. Many single unskilled factory workers and longshoremen lived in furnished one-room units. These rooms rented on a weekly basis were found in mid-size town houses mainly located in the downtown area of Hoboken. A relatively small element of Hoboken's real estate market; however, they provided housing for as many as three hundred mainly male individuals residents.

Delia wrote about the pressure of gentrification, which increased in the 1970s, with furnished single-room-occupancy apartments falling under more scrutiny on the part of the city code officials who viewed these real estate units as akin to transient housing like hotels. This newer perspective was fueled by the economic gentrification forcing the closure of all single-room rentals except for existing hotels and the YMCA. This affected a diverse sector of Hoboken and contributed to the homeless population. Gentrification by fire, fear, intimidation, and economics was recognized by the clergy as one of their responsibilities to serve and care for the poor. This led to the fervent discussions among Hoboken clergy who organized and led the effort to address the growing need. Initially, food pantries, soup kitchens, and temporary shelters were implemented in various churches. This ultimately led to the creation of a homeless shelter by the Clergy Coalition locating at St. John's Lutheran Church on Third and Bloomfield Street. The shelter was dedicated in the name of Bishop John Mahurter of the North American Old Roman Catholic Church, an ordained clergyman whose mission in life was to serve the poor.

St. John's Church, under the leadership of Pastor Triffel Felske, was selected by the coalition, and the church council accepted the calling to serve growing homeless male population initially. The shelter relied on volunteers and community donations for its existence to operate and seek government funding as an incorporated not-for-profit entity. Nevertheless, the shelter's challenges were not limited to funding, but rather faced the city's zoning law as an obstacle to remain open, resulting into a court case. The clergy coalition took the position that St. John's Church had a right under the law to exist as a religious entity serving the poor, which was a basic tenet of Judeo-Christian ethics. Furthermore, the existence of St. John's Church building for over 120 years, the oldest church building in Hoboken, grandfathers the work of the church including serving the poor.

Judge Burrell Ives Humphreys from the Hudson County superior court heard the case. The city requested the court to authorize the shelters closure as they claimed it violated zoning laws. The coalition believed the separation of church and state granted them the authority to operate the shelter bypassing the local zoning law. Judge Humphreys sided with the coalition, allowing them to continue with operating the shelter with the condition safety measures, including fire codes would need to be implemented.

The case covered and reported by Delia provided the foundation for the shelter to be recognized formally by the state, federal, and local governments. Through various funding sources, the shelter moved from only volunteers to full-time staff and a more diverse volunteer cadre. In addition, the target population had expanded from only men to include women as well. All residents who used the facility were called guest as a form of dignity. The shelter population grew from fifty residents to one hundred within the first two years and almost every night it seemed they had to turn away homeless people.

Delia examined the homeless population that used the shelter and found these Hoboken residents were from diverse sectors including senior citizens, young people, men, and women. The shelter did not allow children to stay but did provide meals for all who were in need. The reasons for homelessness were extensive and included former well-employed individuals who found themselves in need of resources to pay the increasing rents. Others were homeless because of family separation, mental illness, veterans with PTSD, drug and alcohol abuse with all directly affected by gentrification. The shelter had taken on the role of social workers and added housing placement as one of their goals.

Delia also came to recognize that a large segment of the homeless population was not being counted because they were housed by family or friends. The doubling up of families in a single apartment became a common occurrence throughout Hoboken, which was called under housed homeless families. However, this category did not receive the same overt attention as a homeless person living in a shelter. Gentrification has coerced the doubling of families in Hoboken and elsewhere, a homeless population rarely counted.

St. Mary's Hospital

St. Mary's Hospital had been serving the community of Hoboken since the 1860s. Originally tending to the Civil War wounded, it was, and remains, a medical center since its start in 1863. Founded by the Franciscan Sisters of the Poor, St. Mary's was a charitable hospital serving all residents regardless of their income. As a hospital, they thrived for one hundred years in a challenging economy because many of its staff were nuns devoted to their calling, which made it financially possible to exist.

The fires of Hoboken in the 1970s and 1980s had many casualties who were injured, and in some cases DOA. The fatalities brought to the hospital required a doctor to pronounce the time and date of the death. During the period of 1973–1982, St. Mary's Hospital healed thousands of people and tended to the sixty-seven residents who died in tenement fires, most of whom were children. The hospital was a safe haven for the surviving fire victims, and the doctors as well as nurses were the heroic staff of angels.

Delia knew how St. Mary's provided primary care for many in the community that did not have health insurance. The blue-collar residents relied on them for pediatric care, emergency care, and was the birth site of most Hobokenite. However, on January 21, 1979, Hoboken experienced its worst fatal tenement fire in history with twenty-one people dying and twenty-one injured with most treated at St. Mary's Hospital. That evening, Delia, who was present at the Clinton Street fire, also walked the block to St. Mary's looking to observe the processing of the injured and DOA. She was very moved to see the families affected by the fire. The injured included some who had jumped from windows and others who dropped babies from windows to their safety. Based on her observation, she concluded that an article should be written about the important role St. Mary's played in Hoboken's past and present, especially during the fires. The article she envisioned would also focus on the medical staff whose commitment to heal was unequivocally achieved under the most difficult moments.

In preparing the article about St. Mary's, Delia chose to interview an emergency nurse Jenifer Gale who had worked there for twenty years. She was able to get a quote from Nurse Gale: "It is the saddest day in my career at St. Mary's Hospital treating the fire victims and knowing that most of the fatalities were children." Unfortunately, the greatest lost at the 131 Clinton Street fire was experienced by the Rampersad-Drepaul family, losing seventeen members, the majority being children. Delia's coverage of the fire and the article about St. Mary's she believed would bring focus to the important role the hospital played in Hoboken. Between the two major fires in 1973 and 1979, thirty-three residents had been killed and hundreds in need of medical services were addressed at St. Mary's. It seemed like a steady stream of fire victims and injured firefighters counted on the hospital and their staff. Finally, based on her discussion with the medical staff members, they were aware of the housing pressures that existed in Hoboken and condemned gentrification by fire.

Delia's article about St. Mary's was encouraged by her editor, John Newton, and was placed on the front page. She described St. Mary's Hospital as Hoboken's safe haven regardless of race, ethnicity, or economic status. She also knew the hospital was always in need of financial help, receiving subsidies from state, federal, and local governments. This concern about St. Mary's future was constantly debated by the hospital board and staff. Simply put, the economic challenge were mounting with the cost of staff, upkeep of the building, and need for new medical equipment. Like many medical centers throughout the United

States, St. Mary's was constantly seeking funds to meet its budgetary obligation. Delia ended her article not only praising the hospital, but also alerting the community that a loss of St. Mary's Hospital would be devastating to the future of Hoboken.

Esperanza (Hope)

Lost does not have to stay forever in grief
Life has given us hope as its relief
The winds of fire did take its toll
    Our hearts filled with maladies we never forget
Tainos taught us to live forever forward
Absence does not make us extinct
We live in the streets, houses and homes
departed
    Our hearts broken by disappointments
But hope lives forever in our visions and
dreams
We left our homes but our hearts and
childhood remain

CHAPTER 24

The Exposé

Delia had now completed all the interviews on her original list and those she added. The task of writing the extensive article was ahead of her. She was confident that the information collected would provide her with a broad perspective on the issues of the fires, fatalities, and gentrification. The calendar was entering February, and she had planned to have a draft ready for Newton by the second week of the month. As per Newton, the draft had to be no more than six paragraphs and included facts that could be verified as well as her opinion.

Writing the exposé was the most challenging effort she would undertake in her career. She knew the article would be read by all sectors of the community and expected a diverse reaction. What was important to her was the truth. Her perceptions would be the voice of those affected by the fires, the families that lost loved ones, and those who were displaced by the gentrification. Yet Delia did not want to write an article that pointed only to those culpable but also provided recommended solutions discerned by the tragedies and the effort needed to prevent them in the future.

After a week of reviewing her notes and writing down points she knew were necessary for the article, Delia began the writing task. The article would be broken into paragraphs describing key elements at different points leading to conclusive recommendations. An effective introduction would draw her readers into the article by touching on the tragedy's numbers affiliated with the saga. The question she struggled with was making it personal with details leading the readers to think of its consequences.

Her second consideration was to share perspectives based on the interviews. The first part would be the city officials describing their thoughts on the issue. It would need to have accurate quotes and interpretations. The following components included the firefighters and police perspective. These two entities were keys to understand the lack of closure, an important factor. In considering the next paragraph, she needed to internalize how the information provided by the insurance investigator, Mr. Guzman, had shared with her. It was the most important and thought-provoking information she had compiled. Yet the delivery of controversial revelations needed a careful approach. She struggled with how to communicate the insight Guzman shared about the FBI choice, the present investigations, and the veracity of his information. This paragraph would prove to be the most arduous one to write.

Delia also believed it had to include elements of Garcia's interview on tenants' rights and Mrs. Torres's heart-tugging interview. Garcia believed gentrification by fire, intimidation, fear, and the fatalities impacted all tenants. His predictions were also future portends of erosions to tenant rights. Finally, Mrs. Torres's poignant story required Delia to be sensitive in capturing the inner thoughts and experiences of their tragedy as seen by the children.

The last paragraph or summary she knew needed to be realistic, practical, and written in a nonpontificating manner. This would be akin to the editorial aspect of the article with recommendations to be considered by city officials, tenants, landlords, developers, and all residents. It was certainly a tall task to reach all listed, but she believed a comprehensive approach was imperative less the article would fall short of its goal.

By the end of February, Delia had completed the draft to submit to Newton. She believed it contained all the points needed to reach the readers. Newton received the draft and told her he would review it and let her know his impression. Newton reminded her that the article would need to be approved by the editorial board members since the premise was in an editorial format.

He told her, "First, I will review, give you feedback, and then it would be presented with any adjustments needed."

"Thank you, I could not have done it without your support."

*****

The following day Newton called Delia to his office to give her his initial feedback.

"I think your article was well-written and does provide the reader with a comprehensive perspective regarding the topic. I do, however, have to make some recommendations for your consideration. Know that the recommendations from my perspective are designed to get the board's approval. However, as the author, you may not agree. First, the FBI choice reference. I think is difficult to substantiate and would receive resistance by the law department. Secondly, the singling out of elected officials and others may not be in the best interest of the newspapers' working relationship. So, considering these two recommendations, let me know how you feel about proceeding to the editorial board."

"Newton, I feel strongly about the article as written. We are talking about fires with fatalities and gentrification which affected thousands of people. Please allow me to stay with the draft and submit it as is to the board. I will be more than happy to attend the meeting and defend the draft."

"Delia, it's not done that way. The draft copy has to have my endorsement prior to submitting it. You are one of the most talented reporters I've worked with, but you have to remember the *Dispatch* is a business as well."

"I understand. Let me look at it again and consider the changes."

Delia left the office with a dejected feeling.

A week later she asked to see Newton with her revised copy. She had eliminated names of elected officials, but rather described them in general terms. Regarding the FBI reference, she felt strongly that it needed to remain in the article. Newton accepted the copy and assured her he would submit it to the editorial board for their consideration. The next board meeting was scheduled for the third week in March.

Delia asked, "If it was approved, when would it be published?"

"In all probability, within weeks of approval."

By weeks end, Newton presented Delia's article to the board who had received it the day before to review. At the meeting, he expressed his support for the article and appealed for their endorsement. However, the board, overall, was not receptive. They believed the *Dispatch* prior editorial, which appeared the previous year, was sufficient. The last fatal fire in Hoboken was six months prior, and the board felt the issue had reached its apex. Newton recognized the lack of support for the article as not meeting their interest at this time. He did however get a commitment from them to reconsider the issue if necessary.

The next day he met with Delia with the bad news explaining to her their apprehension to publish the article at this time but left the door open. She was disappointed and angered by the board's decision. She thanked Newton for his support and left his office disillusioned.

At this point she felt it was time for her to consider leaving the *Dispatch*, where she had spent four years as a reporter. Delia's disappointment was hurtful to her, but she did not lose site of the *Dispatch*'s commitment to her reporting. The change she envisioned would coincide with the fact her parents had planned to retire and move to Orlando, Florida.

Delia saw Maria over the weekend and informed her she would be seeking new employment shortly and asked her to type her new resume. They went over what should appear in the resume and how to proceed including who should receive the resume. She planned to submit it to job employment agencies in New York City known to have headhunter employment agents. Finally, she would send a resume to one of her mentors at the *Globe*, John Mackie, an award-winning reporter. He had started as a reporter at the *Globe* and moved up to his present position as one of the city editors. Delia told Newton of her intension and expressed her appreciation for the opportunity provided by the *Dispatch*, but it was time to move on.

Newton understood and said, "Sometimes the time to leave a setting comes at a junction, I think yours has arrived. I don't blame you, I don't want to lose you, but I understand. Please provide me with a formal letter of resignation delineating your timeline so we can plan for your replacement."

Delia informed Newton that she would be leaving the *Dispatch* by June 1, giving her some time to help her parents who had planned to move the first week of June as well. The other consideration in her timeline would be for her to move in to her new one-bedroom apartment at Applied Housing. The hope and plan on her part was a new job, new apartment, and the next chapter in her life.

By the first week in April, her resume was in full circulation among several media entities in New York City. However, an unexpected phone call would change her plans. John Mackie from the *Boston Globe* called her and made an offer for her to return this time as a senior reporter. He found her resume to be very compelling and said, "Your experience meets our needs here at the *Globe*. We want you to join us." He did go on to offer her a senior reporting position, working with him at the city desk, explaining that Boston was going through gentrification that coincided with her experience. Delia shared with him her time-line and indicated she would be available by mid-June. Mackie asked her to come up to Boston the following week to conclude their discussion and begin her search for an apartment. She basically accepted the offer that included a higher salary than what she earned at the *Dispatch*.

Delia's return to Boston and meeting with Mackie was a refreshing moment for her. The meeting went well, establishing her acceptance of the offer, confirming the starting date, and beginning her search for an apartment. She knew the rents in downtown Boston would be out of her reach, so she hopped on the Boston transit T to Cambridge and rented a one-bedroom apartment close to the MIT station. She treated herself by staying overnight at the Charles Hotel and called both her parents and Maria, confirming her moves. The following day she returned to Hoboken thinking about all the logistics pending in front of her.

First thing Monday morning, she wrote her resignation letter submitting it to Newton. Some of the staff felt she had overreacted to her article not being accepted; but she knew, as well as Newton, it was a natural break for her to seek employment at a larger new company. Newton had informed the human resource office of the pending move, and they had set in motion to replace Delia. Several candidates were being considered by Newton, and she anticipated the replacement would have time to transition with her. The starting date was targeted for mid-May, giving the new reporter time to become acclimated with her help.

Delia reflected on how the last four weeks of April was a whirlwind time in her life. However, little did she know that the evening of April 30 would mark yet another milestone in the saga facing the community. That evening the Pinter, a small hotel located on Fourteenth Street in Hoboken, experienced a fatal fire. The Pinter had housed displaced fire victims' families and was pending its sale to a condominium developer. In a matter of minutes, the building was engulfed with smoke and flames, an obvious sign of arson. The tragedy that unfolded was horrendous claiming twelve lives that evening. Delia, who lived only three blocks from the Pinter Hotel, covered the story for the *Dispatch*. She stayed looking at the fire and knowing the tragedy included yet again low-income families who had sought a safe shelter for their children.

The plight of Hoboken's tragedy had returned again on April 30, 1982. Delia, like many residents, hoped and prayed that this infamy would have ended. Nevertheless, she was remotivated to approach Newton about publicizing her expose article. Two days after the Pinter fire, she submitted her article on the fire and requested to see Newton.

Newton called her into his office and preempted her pitch by saying, "I am submitting your article and expect the board will approve it. I, like many others, never thought or expected for it to happen again. As I told you when we originally discussed the article, you will have takers who will embrace your perspectives and others who will criticize you for it. The most important aspect is the truth. The editorial board meeting is tomorrow, and I will let you know their decision as soon as I know."

Delia left Newton's office with the feeling it would finally get published, unfortunately it took another tragic fatal fire.

The following morning Newton called Delia and informed her that the board had approved the article with some minor suggestions. They were recommending that those entities and individuals who could be called heroes be recognized in the article. Delia accepted their input and readied the article for print.

The Exposé

Dear Readers,

I have served as a reporter for the *Hudson Dispatch* the last four years covering local news and in particular the Hoboken fires. The *Dispatch* has extended this opportunity for me to write a comprehensive article designed to capture the challenges which have faced our community related to the hundreds of fires. These fires have resulted in 67 residents in the last ten years dying in fires, with most of the fatalities as a result of arson. From 1973 to the present, these fires not only included fatalities, but they also contributed to the overall gentrification displacing thousands of residents to move from Hoboken. Fires, fear, intimidation and greed disguised as a business model has been called progress, yet it is a morally challenged paradigm.

Those that blame the low-income families solely for the fires and fatalities suggest a false and cruel narrative. If that premise were true, then the Housing Authority and Applied Housing should be in ashes since their overwhelming populations is low income and majority Puerto Rican families. Our responsibility as a society is to provide children with the opportunity to live free of fear and fire. Benign neglect on the part of local, county and state officials have allowed landlords to ignore violations, tenement buildings to be absent of fire prevention measures such as smoke detectors, fire extinguishers, secured front doors and/or self-closing apartment doors. The fact is the lack of political will has hampered these proactive fire preventive measures which are effective and without a doubt would have saved lives.

The perpetrators of arson need to be apprehended whether they are criminals for hire, landlords, tenants or revenge motivated individuals. Law enforcement also needs to step up to apprehend the culprits responsible for the fatalities and insurance fraud. The lack of Federal law enforcement involvement limited the ability to resolve these cases. In addition, why the FBI as part of the Justice Department did not open a civil rights case is puzzling as it appears a civil rights violation did in fact occur.

The reality is gentrification has prevailed over tenant rights fueled by greed and indifference to low- and moderate-income families. When for sale signs read, "Will Deliver Vacant," knowing there are tenants still occupying the building, one must ask why? Furthermore, the authors of the state regulations on condo conversions never imagined the pressures it placed on tenants as they have in Hoboken. The federal government pivoting away from affordable housing subsidies beginning in 1981, hurt not only low-income tenants, but also moderate-income families looking to improve their lot in life. The development of affordable housing via Applied Housing and other affordable housing entities was the only attempt to balance against gentrification, it has basically come to a halt.

In examining the big picture, I would be remised if those who went beyond the pale to help the victims were not recognized. Tenants who took it upon themselves to have fire watches in their buildings deserve recognition for the initiative.

The firefighters who braved the blaze and saved lives while doing their responsibility including removing the fatalities remains in a dignified manner. Some first responders were police officers who ran into burning buildings to alert the tenants and save lives. The teachers who met their traumatized students comforted them and shared in the loss of other students. Fire victims helped by their neighbors and family members who took in the displaced families were fortunate to have them in their lives. Finally, the clergy who provided spiritual and emotional support for the families who lost loved ones and their homes. Furthermore, their intent on creating a homeless shelter in Hoboken is also heroic. Heroes come in different shapes, forms and are recognized by their action.

Where does Hoboken go from here? Aristotle once said, "Greed has no boundaries," but we do not have to accept his premise. As a city we can do better, landlords can do the right thing for tenants and as good neighbors we can reach out to others in need. Ladies and gentlemen, I appeal to your better nature not just to find fault in the tragedies, but rather find redemption in our actions.

Delia Delgado,
The *Hudson Dispatch*

The Feedback

The article appeared in the May 1 *Dispatch* issue, a Monday, the largest circulation day of the week. Within a few days, the feedback was swift, and as Newton had predicted. Most of them were positive, supporting the need for the fatal fires to end. Others, however, took exception to her perspective and her indirect condemnations. Newton prepared a brief summary of six feedback highlights and critiques, forwarding it to Delia.

THIS IS A ZERO SUM SOCIETY, GET USED TO IT. THIS MEANS THERE ARE WINNERS AND LOSERS, FIGURE IT OUT.

YOUR PERCEPTIONS OF OUR COMMUNITY'S INACTION IS REAL AND THIS NEEDS TO CHANGE.

PROGRESS DOES NOT HAPPEN WITHOUT PAIN.

THE FIRES WERE TRAGIC AND A BLEMISH TO HOBOKEN'S HISTORY.

THE ARTICLE WAS AN OVER DRAMATIC PIECE MEANT TO OFFEND US, IT FAILED.

YOUR EXPOSÉ DESCRIBED THE PUERTO
RICAN COMMUNITY'S STRUGGLE BUT OUR
SPIRIT CANNOT BE DESTROYED.

Delia's review of the critiques encouraged her because both pros and cons meant the article motivated discussion and hopefully action. She received accolades from her colleagues, who concurred with her assessments. This feedback was happening at the same time she was preparing to leave the *Dispatch*.

The last two weeks in May were an emotional roller coaster for her: a high, with the publishing of the article, and mixed feelings, as she prepared to leave the *Dispatch*, her friend Maria, Hoboken, and her parents. Her last day included a coffee at the *Dispatch* conference room with colleagues extending praise. She had worked at the *Dispatch* for approximately four years and wrote many articles about the fires as well as gentrification. She was happy to leave for a larger venue, adding to her career, but leaving the *Dispatch* was also bittersweet.

After the coffee, Maria helped Delia clear her desk and ready to exit as an employee for the last time.

Newton asked her into his office and told her, "It was a pleasure having you at the *Dispatch*. You brought with you new energy to our staff and the courage to fight for what you believed was right. You are a credit to your parents, culture, and profession."

She left his office in tears and smiles.

Political Will

Where a political figure elected or not is willing to commit precious time, energy, funds or capital to achieve and effectuate change. Conversely, when these same players do not show interest or chose inaction when change is needed.

CHAPTER 25

Seeking Justice

Leaving the *Dispatch* was viewed by Delia as a positive move for her career and life goal. She believed that her role at the *Dispatch* as a reporter covering the fires and gentrification in Hoboken was a commitment that transcended to a calling. Yet she felt as a community member more could have been done. Simply, closure for those who lost family members and thousands who were affected by gentrification deserved more. This got her thinking on how she could leave Hoboken and still address the issue of closure. Ultimately, she concluded that one remedy could be to explore the possibility of a class-action lawsuit. Along these lines, she reached out to a nonprofit law group in Washington, D.C., which specialized in housing discrimination and civil rights violations.

Delia had learned of the Housing Justice Group while she was an intern at the *Boston Globe*. She remembered they had represented a large tenant group who were challenging a developer's effort to convert their building into a condominium. The law group was able to secure buyout payments and/or buy-ins on part of tenants. They also had cases involving civil rights violations and inaction on part of the Civil Rights/Justice Department forcing them to act. She believed they could bring a case against the city and county for allowing the systemic removal of thousands of low-income tenants of a minority group.

Delia arranged for an appointment in their Washington, D. C., office to present her argument for a case. Just two weeks prior to her departure from the *Dispatch*, she met with a group of three attorneys who served as a screening committee to identify cases they would undertake. She was led into a conference room where she met with Mr. James Stafford, the case manager, and two other attorneys Ms. Michele Grant and Linda West.

"Good morning, Ms. Delgado. We represent the Law Center's screening committee and will hear your case."

"Yes, thank you for this opportunity. As you are aware I am presently a reporter for the *Hudson Dispatch* but will be leaving on June 1. However, I am here as a private citizen and can be viewed as a former reporter. I have covered the fires and gentrification of Hoboken, New Jersey, for the past four years and have been deeply distressed by what many in the community call inaction, benign neglect on part of the city and county. For the past ten years, sixty-seven people were killed in tenement fires, most of which were children, and over six hundred fires have occurred in this one-mile square city. I also have a copy of demographic reports which show the transient pattern of Puerto Rican families who were forced to move from Hoboken. The fact is accountability and closure for these events were never established. The community is asking for justice especially for those who died in arson fires and thousands who were forced out by fear, fire, and intimidation. That's a synopsis of the case in hope that it may be accepted."

She was referring to the summary she had previously submitted to the committee.

"Although I am not an attorney, I did some research into the civil rights laws and believe there are relevant provisions which directly correspond to what has happened in Hoboken. Between the 1964 and 1968 civil rights laws, there are terms, and I paraphrase, 'It is illegal to discriminate, threaten, coerce, intimidate or interfere with anyone exercising a fair housing right.' I think the Civil Rights office should have acted under this and other elements of the law requiring them to initiate an investigation. In addition, in many other situations, a hostile environment existed for tenants violating the Title 8 Fair Housing Act by harassing them to leave impacting a community of a single race, color, or national origin. I characterize the exit of thousands of Puerto Rican families as being proverbially escorted out of the city and their homes."

"Ms. Delgado, thank you for your presentation. I see you have brought with you some documentation or data that would support your claim."

"Yes, I have put together several folders of articles on the fires and gentrification, not only from the *Dispatch*, but others as well."

"Ms. Delgado, if we were to consider it, we would need a group of people who were directly involved in the situation including parents of children who perished in the fires, families who were intimidated to move, and others equally affected. Do you think it is possible to assemble such a group? Quite frankly, without their direct involvement, we could not proceed with a case. Now, as I have stated earlier, this committee must evaluate all the data possible to determine whether we will proceed. If the committee agrees to proceed, a research effort will be undertaken to collect relevant information from the community. Once the data is collected and studied, then and only then the decision to move forward would be made. Understood?"

"Yes, it seems time-consuming to reach a decision, but I understand the protocol. I have secured a commitment from a tenant group, which would serve as the contacts. Mr. John Garcia heads a nonprofit group in Hoboken and would provide the complainants."

"Ms. Delgado, would you be one of the complainants?"

"Well, it depends on you. I would be glad to serve as one of the groups, but I will be moving to Boston shortly."

"If and when we get to that point, the attorneys will decide what role you can play, even from Boston. Thank you, Ms. Delgado, we will get back to you by next week with a preliminary determination."

Delia left the law center office with a positive vibe with the hope that they would consider the case. It was a feeling that her exit from Hoboken would not be in vain and include this effort at justice.

A week later Delia received a call from Mr. Stafford, saying, "Delia, I just want to let you know the Center completed the screening committee review. It was well debated for its merit and the impact which the Puerto Rican community went through these past years. You need to know your presentation was compelling enough for the committee to continue evaluating it. Having said that, they continue to question the ability to formulate a case. I will be sending you an outline of informational inquiries that need to be answered. Let me say this, I have reviewed many cases at the Center in the past. I do want you to know, I support the case to move forward on its merit. Once the data requested is submitted, in all probability, a case worker will be assigned. You should know since you will be leaving Hoboken, the key to proceeding with the case would rely mainly on a point person. Do you have any questions for me at this time?"

"Mr. Stafford, thank you for your call. It's the most promising effort I have heard toward achieving closure. When will I receive the Center's inquiries?"

"I will overnight it today, and you should receive it tomorrow at the *Dispatch*, so look out for it."

"The minute I receive it, I will get started. Thank you for all your help."

Delia did receive the package the following day and began to review the outline describing what had to be done. She felt it was important to tell Newton what she had done to pursue the Center's involvement. She explained, although she was an employee for one more week, she believed no ethical rules were violated since a case if it is developed would occur after her exit from the *Dispatch*. She did, however, commit to Newton that if a case is filed, the *Dispatch* would be the first to know.

The day after leaving the *Dispatch*, Delia got started on the inquiries from the Center. She needed to establish who would be the point person and immediately called John Garcia to request his involvement as the lead. Mr. Garcia, who knew she was pursuing this action, agreed to serve as the lead and secure the other complainants including parents of children who died in the fires. Delia arranged a conference call with Mr. Stafford, John Garcia, and herself. They established the working relationship that would be needed to proceed, and Mr. Stafford explained that pressure would be placed by the city on them to withdraw from the case if it materializes. Plainly speaking, Stafford wanted to know if Garcia was strong enough to hold the line and not fold under pressure. Stafford indicated that a staff researcher would be assigned and spent time in Hoboken with him and the others who would be involved. Mr. Garcia stated he understood the responsibility and committed to stay strong until an acceptable resolution is achieved. What would be acceptable would be defined by the complainants, the Center attorneys, and, ultimately, the city. The final question in the Center's letter was along the line of closure. They wanted to know what would constitute it and how committed they were to achieve it.

Delia was concerned about the time it would take in preparing the response to the Center since she had basically three weeks before leaving to Boston.

The following day she met with Mr. Garcia to schedule a meeting with the group that would be the complainants. At the meeting, they established the potential for a case that would hold the city and county accountable for their ineffective action against the fires and fatalities. That evening, six people were identified as complainants: Mr.

Garcia as a tenant advocate; Ms. Torres representing the families displaced by the fires; Mr. Raymond Young, who lost two family members in the fires; Jose Torres, the son of Ms. Torres who represented the children; Mr. Milton Ortiz, a senior citizen representative; and Delia Delgado.

The final topic that needed to be discussed was the demands that would be included as part of the lawsuit. Delia asked the committee to think about it over the weekend and return on Monday prepared to address the topic: closure. On Monday, without hesitation, the topic was presented, with Delia indicating the demand would have to focus on the Hispanic community, low-income tenants, the families who lost loved ones, and the children. Mr. Garcia had prepared a list for the committee to consider, which included monetary settlements for families who lost loved ones; a commitment by the city of Hoboken to provide affordable housing for families who were displaced, giving them priority; and finally a dedicated park or building that would recognize the tragedy into the future, never to be forgotten. The committee agreed to the list and took a moment to reflect on its impact. Delia prepared the response to the Center with the lawsuit demands and the complainants names and addresses including hers.

The following week Mr. Stafford called Delia to inform her that the application was formally approved for the next step with the researcher's assignment. She informed him that Mr. Garcia should be the person to receive all communications about the case. In closing, she thanked Mr. Stafford again and said, "Closure was in his hands."

With the acceptance by the law center to proceed with the research and file a lawsuit, Delia believed she had accomplished her goal and moved to Boston knowing she planted the seed for closure.

*****

Three weeks into her new job at *Boston Globe*, Delia received a package from the *Hudson Dispatch*. Upon opening it, she saw a letter from Newton and additional paperwork. Newton wrote to inform her she was nominated for a Pulitzer Prize in the category of a new reporter. The application copy enclosed identified her work on the Hoboken fires and gentrification, citing over fifty articles, including the exposé. Delia was humbled and flattered by the jester on the part of Newton and the *Dispatch*.

Newton wrote, "You are an inspiration for all reporters, and it was an honor to have nominated you."

Two months later, she heard from the Pulitzer organization informing her that the application, although with merit, was not selected. Delia nevertheless felt proud to have been considered and forwarded copies of the correspondence to her parents in Orlando, Florida.

EPILOGUE

The loss of sixty-seven residents to fires from 1973–1982 is a tragic saga in the history of Hoboken. Hundreds of fires occurred during this period culminating in fatalities and/or the displacements of families from their homes. Thousands were forced out of their homes by gentrification by fire, intimidation, fear, or economics. This dilemma lacked the attention it deserved on the part of civic leaders and residents. Lives could have been saved by a more proactive initiative to retrofit tenement buildings with smoke detectors, fire extinguishers, and meaningful investigations. The author utilized media data, research, and his past experiences in writing this historic saga.

The goal of the author was to contribute facts and conjectures to the literature. He facilitated the historic moments utilizing a fictitious character to guide us through this time. Delia Delgado represented the average young person who grew up in Hoboken with dreams of success and happiness. Her parents, like thousands of Hoboken residents, was part of the diaspora from Puerto Rico seeking a better life for themselves and their families. Delia, a talented writer in high school, pursued a career in journalism, seeking to shed light on truth and knowledge in our society. An UMASS Boston graduate, her experiences made her the perfect storyteller with a broad perspective challenging the reader to seek the truth about befallen.

Befallen was selected as the title because it describes the inequitable burden placed on the families whose only fault was being poor. This attribute does not mean they were absent of aspirations or goals in life. They were poor, and English was not their first language. But the children had hope, love, and families, never to be forgotten. The fortunate do have responsibility to society helping their neighbors and families. This challenge is presented to all of us as readers and a community to help the befallen.

God Always Shines on the Puerto Rican People

The culture, food, music, and prayers have always delivered us from our challenges

Hurricanes, droughts, or fires have hampered our spirit forward can be our only step

Many are poor but not despaired

We lift our lives when it gets very low rebounding in strength and resolve

Complexities are present in our every-day from Island to mainland we represent

Stand for what is right our responsibility is never spent

Citizens, veterans, teachers, police officers, fire fighters and clerks too many others to name that works

Business and law we stand for the best, doctors, researchers, and scientists as well

God does shine on the Puerto Rican people do tell

THE BEFALLEN

The following is the actual names of sixty-seven Hoboken residents who died in the fires from 1973–1982. As presented in the book, accountability was never achieved, leaving families and the community absent of closure. The majority of the deceased were children, seventeen years to one month. What is missing from the list is the countless individuals injured in the hundreds of fires during this period and the thousands displaced as a result of gentrification by fire.

The Fatal Fires

Dates	Addresses	Deceased	Age
September 2, 1973	263 Eleventh Street	Carlos Lopez	50
		Francisca Lopez	50
		Patricia Raquena	19
		JacaquelineRaquena	18
		Canola Raquena	16
		Juana Requena	14
		Gladys Santos	Unknown
		Dionisio Santos	10
		Milissa Santos	7

		Janet Santos	3
		Carlo Santos	8
March 10, 1978	360 Marshal Drive	Alberto Langini	40
May 6, 1978	70 Washington Street	Julia Rodriquez	Unknown
		Jesus Rodriquez	Unknown
January 20, 1979	131 Clinton Street	GayatriRampersad	35
		Sandra Rampersad	12
		Indravati Rampersad	11
		Bholaram Rampersad	10
		Inder Rampersad	8
		Fatbay Rampersad	7
		Sharmun Rampersad	4
		Neclavati Rampersad	2
		Jacob Drepani	43
		Gangapati Depani	39
		Roxanne Drepani	17
		Andrian Drepani	15
		Mukesh Drepani	13
		Veronica Drepani	11
		Raymond Drepani	9
		Premnath Drepani	6
		Pradeep Drepani	5
		Nicholas Torres	24
		Maria T. Torres	17
		Margarita Torres	16
		Marilyn Torres	14

Date	Address	Name	Age
October 25, 1979	311 First Street	Edna Gadea	39
		Tawary Colon	1
October 20, 1980	224 Jefferson Street	Louis Sanchez	8
		Victor Sanchez	2
October 12, 1981	67 Park Avenue	Javier Galicia	2
		Modesto Galicia	7
October 25, 1981	102 Twelfth Street	Goduvim Mercado	34
		Ana Mercado	35
		Ruth Mercado	13
		Dennise Mercado	12
		Walter Mercado	10
		Kenneth Mercado	9
		Manuel Vega	76
		Remeira Rios	43
		Frank Rios	20
		Marybell Rios	18
		Jesus Rios	13
November 21, 1981	80 Rivers Street	Walter Mitchell	51
	(American Hotel)	Howard Warshaver	52
April 30, 1982	151 Fourteenth Street	Anna H. Perez	45
	(Pinter Hotel)	Francisca Vasquez	41
		Juan Serrano	38

Olga Garcia	22
Luz D. Garcia	17
Ismael Vasquez	15
Angel L. Perez	8
Luis X. Colon	4
Charles Serrano	3
Jorge Negron	8 months
Catherine Torres	6 months
Erica Negron	1 month
Maria Colon	20

Note: Names compiled by the Hoboken Historic Museum and the author.

Closure

A culmination of an experience or situation bringing it to an end creating the opportunity for a new start.

REFERENCES

The following are the references utilized by the author in writing *Befallen*.

Books and Documents:

- *Ladies and Gentlemen, the Bronx Is Burning* (Johnaton Mahler)
- *The Power Broker* (Robert A. Caro)
- "Hoboken Is Burning" (research paper) (Dylan Gotlieb)
- "Vanishing Hoboken" (a series of the Hoboken Oral History Project, Hoboken Historic Museum)
- "The Fire House" (recollections of Bill Bergin)
- "And Then I Started Reading Books" (recollections of Maria Peggy Diaz)
- *Yuppies Invaded My House at Dinner Time* (Joseph Barry and John Derevlany, eds.)
- *Delivered Vacant* (a film documentary) (Nora Jacobson)

Graphic Art Presentation:

- "The Fires: Hoboken 1978–82" (Chris Lopez)

Print Media Articles:

- *Jersey Journal*
- *Hudson Dispatch*
- *Star-Ledger*
- *New York Times*
- *Daily News*
- *Hoboken Reporter*

Other References:

- Jersey City, Hoboken and South Amboy Public Libraries
- Hoboken Historic and Fire House Museum
- Miracle Mile Mirror, 1971

Quotes:

- "Grace under pressure" (Ernest Hemingway)
- "Four Freedoms" (Franklin D. Roosevelt)
- "Ladies and gentlemen, the Bronx is burning." (Howard Cosell)
- "Show me a hero and I'll write you a tragedy." (F. Scott Fitzgerald)
- "Tale of two cities" (Charles Dickens)
- "Freedom of Fear" (Norman Rockwell) (print)
- "Greed has no boundaries" (Aristotle, Greek Philosopher)

Internet Research:

- Google
- Wikipedia

*Special recognition is extended to my wife, Santa, and niece Autumn Figueroa Grinage for their assistance in editing and formatting.

Courtesy of the Miracle Mile Mirror

ENDORSEMENTS

Hoboken is currently viewed as a fashionable locale, minutes from New York City with coveted brownstones, fancy waterfront condos, fabulous restaurants, boutiques, and an upscale population. Hoboken's history possesses great stories and famous names for whom it can proudly boast. But within Hoboken's unique history lies a shameful story... Edwin Duroy, the author, revisits Hoboken's "dark period" of the 1970s and 80s and opens the door for the reader to understand how ARSON BY DESIGN reshaped the town. Duroy, a longtime resident of the city, devotes countless hours and months to this research. He presents a spellbinding narrative through the voice and actions of a young, novice reporter, Delia Delgado of Hoboken's *Hudson Dispatch*. Through Delia's voice, you can feel the searing heat, smell the pungent odor of scorched flesh, and become privy to the cover-up within all levels of government. Duroy's historical tome is, by far, the most complete and truthful account of this shameful period.

If you think you know Hoboken, this book will open your mind to how it came to be.

Dr. Merry Naddeo,
Retired Educator

Many books can inform you, but *Befallen* will transform your view of the 1970s Hoboken tragedies. Growing up in Hoboken gave me a foundation to succeed in life, but it also gave me memories of lost dreams by the children in the Hoboken fires. Hopefully, the book achieves some closure to the Hispanic community.

Anthony Mestre
Hobokenite

Reading *Befallen*, I was instantly transported back to that fateful night in September 1972, as an eleven-year-old living on Eleventh and Willow Avenue. I looked out my window and witnessed the horrific flames engulfing the buildings across the street, which extinguished the lives of many. It is hard to believe that no one was ever brought to justice for causing such a horrific tragedy.

Ray Perez
Hoboken Resident

Befallen: The Hoboken Fires 1973–1982
Wow!
In reading through the pages of Befallen, I recalled once again those Hoboken years and the events of the Hoboken fires which brought about death, destruction, and displacement of so many individuals and families. Some of us met together to discuss these problems. Members of the

Hoboken clergy joined together to establish a coalition from our various faith communities to address these concerns and needs within our Hoboken community.

The tragic deaths of so many children and adults, as a result of those fires, brought the clergy and some parishioners to gather and publicly pray at each of those sites of horrific destruction. The coalition formed to confront the evil and injustice inflicted on so many people as a result of greed and profit through arson which brought about homeless individuals and families needing food and shelter.

In 1982, the Hoboken Clergy Coalition established the Hoboken Shelter for the Homeless. This newly organized coalition was instrumental in securing the shelter's right to exist, including taking the case to the New Jersey Superior Court, which affirmed the sheltering people in a church is a protected religious freedom.

Bishop Joseph Mahurter of the North American Old Roman Catholic Church lived under Franciscan vows and ran a mission servicing the low-income Hispanic community in Hoboken. He was consecrated in 1969 by Archbishop Huber Rogers and did his university studies in New Brunswick, Canada, at Saint Thomas. He was invited to become a member of the Hoboken Clergy Coalition and worked with the poor and homeless. He died on June 22, 1983, in Hoboken (age sixty-two). Upon his death, the Hoboken Shelter for the Homeless was also named in his blessed memory.

The mission of our community shelter has always been to provide hot meals and warm beds to all people in need.

Now after forty years, additional services and various programs continue to help the poor and needy among us.

Revenant Triffel L. Felske

Unanswered Questions

LIABILITY   CULPABILITY   NEGLIGENCE

These are questions which should have been asked by investigators, reporters, civic leaders, insurance companies and the reader.

1. Who benefited by the fatal fires and who was liable for the deaths?

2. If insurance was paid on the fatal fires deemed arson, who collected the premiums?

3. Were any of the buildings which experienced fatal fires have open violations which could have contributed to the fatalities? Was this negligence?

4. Was the City, County and State aware of open violations and were they addressing it in a timely manner? Were these entities liable for unaddressed violations?

5. Was an effective investigation conducted in any of the fatal fires?

6. Where are the fire and police records for the fatal fires?

7. Did insurance companies conduct their own inves-
    tigations of the fatal fires?

8. Is it correct to say that if arson is a felony, then
    those who were killed in the fatal fires are felony
    murders.
    If so, since murder does not have a statue of limita-
    tion, are these cases still open?

9. Why did the FBI not get involved in the fatal fires
    but were involved with the 1972 Foodtown fire?

These and other questions raised by victims' families,
friends and neighbors need to be answered before closure
can be achieved.

ABOUT THE AUTHOR

Dr. Edwin Duroy was born in Bayamon, Puerto Rico (1950). He was two years old when his family moved to Hoboken, New Jersey. He lived in Hoboken for fifty-two years, where he saw the transformation of the community and its gentrification including the arson fires of the 1970–1980s. He is a retired educator serving as a teacher, administrator, and college professor. Dr. Duroy graduated from Jersey City State College, Montclair State College, and the University of Massachusetts Amherst. He resides with his wife Santa in South Amboy, New Jersey.